The Pony With
No Name

Diana Hallam

The Pony With
No Name

Typeset by Roberta L Melzl
Editor: Bobbie Chase
Printed in Germany, 2009

ISBN: 978-1-934983-29-4
Stabenfeldt, Inc.
225 Park Avenue South
New York, NY 10003
www.pony4kids.com

Available exclusively through PONY.

1: The Thirteenth Pony

Some girls have bedrooms, but Linnea slept in a small pink pony museum. All around the walls were large photos of all the ponies she had ever ridden, in order, since the age of four. Under each photo was a lovingly painted sign with the pony's name. Linnea knew all these names by heart. If ever she couldn't get to sleep at night she would recite them over and over again: Ricky, Pontus, Joker, Nell-Sparkle, Chestnut, Domino, Tom-Trickster, Hampus, Starlight and Patch.

That June morning, however, as she looked at the photos on her wall, Linnea realized that the next pony would be the thirteenth. She felt a stab of anxiety. People said thirteen was an unlucky number, but surely that was superstitious nonsense?

"Linnea!" It was Sam, her younger brother. He came into her room looking worried. "Mom isn't up yet. Do you think we should go in?" Linnea checked her watch. It was ten past eight. Mom usually got up at six. She looked at Sam and hesitated.

"I think we'd better risk it," she said. Mom's bedroom was her cave. She hid there when she needed to be alone. If the door was shut and you went in without good reason, you'd meet a bear.

"Out, out, out!" she would growl. But today there was definitely something wrong.

"Right," said Linnea "I'm going in, but I want you right behind me, okay?" Sam nodded and gulped.

They crept down the corridor, their bare feet making no sound on the smooth birch floor. Linnea put her hand on the doorknob, took a deep breath and stepped into the room. The reading light by the bed was still on, in spite of the sunlight streaming through the windows, and Mom was lying on top of the bed in her clothes from the day before. She was propped up against some pillows but her head sagged back and her mouth was open. She was surrounded by heaps of exam papers and she was snoring.

"I think we'd better wake her up," said Sam.

"Yeah," agreed Linnea. Mom was usually so organized and neat, yet here she lay with yesterday's makeup still on and her glasses askew. What was going on? She nudged her mother's arm and then stood back. Mom woke up immediately but looked startled.

"Oh!" she exclaimed as she glanced down at her pant legs and saw the piles of paper all around, "I've gone to sleep on my work!" She detached her glasses from her right ear and settled them back over her sleepy eyes.

"What time is it?" she asked, yawning.

"Quarter past eight" said Linnea gently.

"What?" shouted Mom. She jumped into the air as if she had just been given an electric shock. "I'm late! Linnea, get breakfast and dress your brother. You'll have to walk him to school today. I've got to be at the university in ten minutes!"

Linnea hustled Sam out of the room and together they started gulping down their cereal. Mom rushed through the kitchen to the front door. She had managed fresh makeup and clean clothes, but breakfast was out of the question.

✳ ✳ ✳

Linnea smiled as she walked through the school gates. It was the last day of the semester so there was a festive atmosphere. She sat next to her best friend Mia in the back of the class and they started to whisper while the English teacher put on a video.

"Are you going to your summer house this year?" Mia asked.

"Yes," replied Linnea. "I'm going to ride Storm."

Mia nodded. She'd heard all about Reingold Stables. Sometimes Linnea talked about nothing else.

"Do you think they'll let you ride him this time?" she asked.

"You two stop gossiping, please," said the teacher. "We can't enjoy the movie if people talk." Linnea winked at her friend and they settled down to watch the video. It was pretty good and much better than a normal English lesson, but Linnea couldn't concentrate. She kept thinking about the beautiful black pony that only the best riders were allowed to try.

"Storm is not for the faint-hearted," Maggie, the instructor, would say every year. "I don't think you're ready yet, Linnea."

"Please!" pleaded Linnea, "Klara is allowed to

ride him and she's six months younger than I am." But Maggie just shook her head.

"You're not ready yet," she would say.

"But when will I be ready?" Linnea had wailed.

"It's hard to say exactly," Maggie would reply, "it just happens and you can't force it." Then Linnea would be filled with irritation. She was the only girl at the riding school who didn't ride all year. Many of the girls lived out in the country and had their own ponies or else they were rich city girls whose moms had the time and money to take them to riding lessons every week. All things considered Linnea did well to keep up at all.

"You've got riding in your bones," Maggie had said last year. "I could see that from the start."

A photo of that day sat in a silver frame next to Mom's bed; Linnea stood next to Ricky, the black Shetland, with a look of rapt concentration as she brushed the pony down. Suddenly the bell rang and jolted Linnea back to the present.

At the end of the school day Linnea slipped through the excited crowds and ran home. Summer vacation! Finally! She reached for the key around her neck and let herself into the apartment. To her surprise Mom was home, slumped over the kitchen table with her face in her arms. She was sobbing.

2: The Pact

"Mom, Mom! What's the matter?" asked Linnea, but Mom just shook her head and kept on crying. "What's wrong?" Linnea asked again.

Now Mom looked up. Tears streamed down her face, carrying small trails of mascara onto her cheeks.

"I've missed the deadline so now I'm not going to get paid."

"But that's not fair," cried Linnea. "You've never been late before."

Mom tried to look brave. "Examiners are paid for each paper they grade," she explained. "I've missed the July deadline so now I'll have to wait till August to get my money."

"Well that's okay then," said Linnea, "you'll get the money in the end."

"Yes, honey," said Mom, "but the money won't come in time for our summer vacation, so I'm afraid we can't go."

She looked up at Linnea, her eyes full of apology. Linnea swallowed hard. She knew that she was about to cry so she dashed to the front door.

"I'm just going out," she croaked. As she swung

around the final corner of the staircase there was a cry. She had knocked Sam to the ground.

"Hey!" he shouted "Look where you're going!" He picked himself up and straightened his backpack. "What's the matter, anyway?"

"The matter?" shrieked Linnea. "You go upstairs and talk to Mom and you'll soon find out what the matter is!" Sam started to hurry upstairs. His backpack was too heavy for him and his pants were too long. Linnea suddenly felt heartbroken for him. He too was going to have a horrible time stuck in the apartment all summer. There had to be a solution, but what could they do? Linnea racked her brain.

"On second thought, don't go upstairs," she said firmly. "Do you have your cell phone?"

Sam nodded.

"Can I have it?"

Linnea leaned against the cool wall of the hallway and began to dial Mom's department at the university.

"What's going on?" asked Sam as he slumped onto the bottom step of the staircase.

"I'm saving our summer vacation," replied Linnea with more confidence than she felt.

"Hello, Social Sciences." It was a man's voice.

"Hello," said Linnea "I'd like to speak to the Head of Department, please."

"This is the Head of Department," came the brisk reply. "Who's calling, please?"

Linnea took a deep breath. "My name is Linnea Karlsson and I'm calling to talk about my mother Karin."

"I see," said the man, "fire away." There was a new note of interest in his voice.

"Well," said Linnea, "she needs to be paid for her grading in July, not August. Otherwise we can't afford to go on vacation." There was a pause at the other end of the line.

"She's never, ever been late for a deadline before," continued Linnea, "and it's hard for her to get things done because she looks after me and my brother on her own."

"So you're not going on vacation with your father?" he asked.

"No," Linnea replied quietly, "we can't go on vacation with Dad." Sam looked at the floor.

"Okay," said the Head of Department. "I'll see what I can do. If I stop by later, will your mom be in?"

"Yes," said Linnea "she's already home but..."

"She doesn't know that you've called me?"

Linnea couldn't think what to say. Suddenly she felt ashamed. Other kids didn't have to do this kind of thing.

"Swift intervention, tact and diplomacy," said the man thoughtfully.

"Sorry?" asked Linnea.

"It's a pact," he said, "I'll see you at six."

Linnea switched the phone off and handed it back to Sam.

"So?" he asked.

"I don't know," she said, "but he's coming at six."

Sam shrugged.

"Footie?" he asked, tilting his head on one side as he always did when he asked a favor.

"Oh, all right." sighed Linnea. They stepped out into the forecourt and Linnea took up her usual position in front of the soccer goal that Sam had chalked onto the parking lot wall. While Sam practiced his penalty shots Linnea traveled in her mind to Reingold Stables. She thought of Storm, sleek and black behind his green stable door. What a haughty horse he was! He didn't seem to care if you pet him or not, and he never nuzzled you for a carrot. He was a machine; precise, accurate and cool, like a top of the line Mercedes. Storm was the ultimate challenge.

"Ouch!" shouted Linnea indignantly as a ball hit the side of her head.

"I can't help it if you don't concentrate," said Sam as the ball bounced back toward him. They played on, stopping from time to time when cars pulled in to park. When she put her mind to it Linnea could block a few of Sam's shots, and Sam loved it whenever she did.

"Good save!" he would shout. He wanted her to get into the game, to enjoy it as much as he did, but they both knew that she only played to please him. Eventually their neighbor, Peter Weinstock, arrived in his battered Volvo station wagon. He parked in front of Sam's makeshift goal and the game came to an end as it always did. Linnea glanced at her watch. It was half past five. Time to get Mom ready for the Head of Department's visit.

They bounded upstairs two at a time and burst into the apartment. There was an ominous silence. Nobody was there.

"Oh, no!" groaned Linnea, "Don't tell me she's gone

out!" A note was tucked under the fruit bowl on the kitchen table. "Gone to Maria's. Back later." Sam flung his bag on the floor in disgust.

"Now what?" he asked. Linnea sat down and put her head in her hands. The chances of Mom getting back from Maria's by six were nil. Her vision of Storm began to blur and fade away.

"We'll just have to tackle the Head of Department on our own," she said. The front doorbell rang and they both instinctively looked at the kitchen clock, but it was still only five thirty. Sam's eyes lit up.

"It's okay!" he shouted, "she's forgotten her keys!" Linnea breathed a sigh of relief. Mom often left her car keys in the pocket of the raincoat that still hung in the hall. She ran to the door and threw it open.

"Mom!" she cried, but a tall man filled the doorway. The first thing that Linnea noticed about him was his very freckled face and his friendly green eyes. He ran his hands nervously through his longish gray-brown curly hair.

"Hello," said Linnea hesitantly, but she made no move to let him in.

"I'm Max O'Leary, from the university," he explained.

"Oh!" said Linnea, startled.

"Is your mom in?" he asked, glancing over her shoulder.

By now Sam had come to the door and was staring at Max thoughtfully.

"No," he said, "she's running late. But you can probably come in anyway."

This jolted Linnea into action. "She'll be back any minute," she lied hurriedly, "Please come in."

"I'm a little early," he said as he settled into an armchair. Sam moved uneasily from one foot to the other and Linnea felt her heart begin to beat faster.

"We'll make you some coffee," she stammered and she dragged her brother into the kitchen and shut the door.

"Get cookies," she hissed, "I'll do the drinks." By the time they emerged Max was happily watching cartoons.

"Oh!" said Linnea in surprise. "Do you like Pink Cat's Parade?"

"Love it," said Max as he bit into a ginger cookie.

Feeling unsure of what to do next, Linnea perched on the end of the sofa. Sam stood warily by.

"Sorry, would you rather watch soccer?" Max asked. "The game's on now." He glanced at Sam and changed channels. Soon they were both glued to the game, shouting instructions to the players.

Half an hour passed and then an hour, but still Mom did not come. Finally, at five past seven the soccer came to an end and Max looked at his watch.

"I'm afraid I can't stay any longer," he said. "It seems as if I won't get to see your mom." Sam and Linnea exchanged glances. "Get to see Mom?" Linnea's mind started to race.

"You could come another time," she said quickly. "How about tomorrow night?"

"I'm afraid not," said Max, "I'm going out of town tomorrow for a conference."

"Oh," said Linnea, beginning to panic. "What are we going to do about Mom's money?"

"I'm afraid I can't do anything about that," said Max.

"But we'll be stuck in the stupid apartment all summer," protested Linnea, " and it's not fair because children need exercise, especially Sam because he's growing and especially me because I only get to ride during summer vacation and this was the year I was finally going to ride Storm." She had been brave with Mom and brave with Sam but now she had no courage left. She wanted to bawl her eyes out.

Max stood up and stroked the back of his neck. He looked at the floor and seemed to be weighing something.

Then he said, "I can't do anything about your mom's deadline, but I have got a dead uncle."

There was a pause while Linnea digested this strange piece of information.

"A dead uncle?" she said.

"Yes, he died three months ago."

"Oh," said Linnea "I'm sorry."

"The dead uncle is no good to you, of course," continued Max.

"No," agreed Linnea, baffled.

"But the thing is, he left me his summer house."

Linnea and Sam held their breaths.

"It's a wreck," said Max, "an absolute disgrace. Needs lots of painting and repairs." He paused. "The work has to be done properly and I don't have any money to pay workmen." He stopped again and looked closely at the children. Linnea felt like a drowning girl who has been

15

thrown a rope. The rope was lying a few feet away from her on the surface of the water. Max seemed to be willing her to reach out and grab it.

"Mom, Sam and I, we do all the painting and repairs in our apartment," she began. Max nodded vigorously, urging her on.

"We could stay at your uncle's place for the summer and fix it up for you," she continued, "but there has to be a riding school. Is there a riding school?"

"Next door," said Max. "Mind you, it's a strange setup. A creepy place, really. But it's better than nothing, I suppose. Do we have a deal?"

"Yes!" chorused the children.

"Right," said Max, "now let's talk about your mom." Something in the way he said this made Sam glance at Linnea again.

"Will you guys persuade her to take my offer?"

They both nodded.

"Good," said Max. "If you will be my allies, I think I've got a strategy.

3: The Summer House

Mom came back at nine, tired and in no mood to talk. When she heard about the new vacation plan she was not pleased.

"How dare you go talking to people we hardly know about our problems?" she shouted. "Have you no shame? What's Max going to think now? That I send my children on begging missions?".

"It wasn't a begging mission," objected Sam, "it was a helping mission."

"For goodness sake," said Mom, "raising you on my own is hard enough. Do you have to humiliate me as well?"

"Why don't you marry Max, then?" suggested Sam. At this point Mom was lost for words. She seemed to be gasping for air. Linnea threw Sam a dark look and then leaped in with the speech that Max had used.

"This is a purely amicable arrangement," she began. "We would be non fee-paying, free, tenant vacation guests in return for free labor, to defray the cost of restoration."

"What are you talking about?" asked Mom. Her eyes

narrowed with suspicion. "Has Max told you to say these things?" Linnea felt herself start to blush. She mustn't give Max away. Best to use her own words now.

"Listen, Mom! Concentrate. We fix up the house for free. In return we get to spend the summer there. It's not charity because the house is a mess and he couldn't rent it for money anyway. Do you get it now?"

"I get it," said Mom.

"I think Max really likes you and he wants you to take the house because he likes you and then he can come and see you and stuff and kiss you maybe," added Sam. Mom blushed crimson. Linnea had never seen her look so embarrassed. Even Sam realized that he might have gone too far.

"I made most of that up," he said quickly.

But Sam's outburst seemed to clinch it.

"We'll go," said Mom. "Max has made a very kind offer and it would be rude to turn him down." And with that she disappeared hurriedly into the kitchen.

✳ ✳ ✳

When Linnea woke the next day she tried not to think about Storm. She threw jeans and T-shirts into her suitcase and then packed her toothbrush, hairbrush and swimsuit.

"I'm just lucky to be going riding at all," she told herself. "It's no good thinking about Reingold now." Then she looked at her battered riding gear in dismay. What if it no longer fit? Mom wouldn't be able to afford replacements this year. She tried not to think about how immaculate Klara always looked and she felt tears of regret and frustration stinging her eyes. Klara would look so classy riding Storm this summer with her brand new boots and shining chestnut hair.

She slipped on her riding things and found that the hat and safety vest still fit. So did the boots, but they were tight. "Anyway it's not how you look, it's how you ride that matters," she told herself. This made her feel miserable again. *I'll never know,* she thought, *I'll never know if I can handle Storm better than Klara.*

With a heavy heart she shuffled into the kitchen for breakfast. This pony craziness was all very well, but it could break your heart if you let it. She forced herself to forget all thoughts of riding. It was time to concentrate on today.

As Mom drove them through the countryside, Linnea started to imagine how bad the uncle's house might be. Would there be holes in the roof? Perhaps there weren't even beds? Mom had packed absolutely everything, just in case.

"We'll pack as if we're going camping," she had said, "and then it won't matter if the house is a ruin." After much list writing and afterthoughts the car was so full that it sank onto its wheels. The sleeping bags stuffed behind the kid's seats made it impossible to see out of the back window. The cans of paint and the folding ladder had taken up more space than anybody had expected. Sam had tried to get Mom to leave them behind so he could fit in his keyboard.

"Forget it, Sam," said Mom. "We've promised Max we'll make his house nice and that is exactly what we're going to do."

Now they left the last big town behind and turned onto a much quieter road flanked on either side by vast cornfields. Barns and farmhouses nestled behind windbreaks of trees. Only villages lay ahead, each with its own whitewashed church and small shop.

"Are we nearly there yet?" Sam asked for the thousandth time.

"This is the village, coming up," said Linnea.

The first thing they saw was an abandoned-looking yellow farmhouse surrounded by grazing ponies. A broken board read, "Farhult Rid. All abilities ca."

"Hey!" yelled Linnea. "That must be the riding school. Mom, can you stop?"

"Can't we just get to the house now? I'm sick of the car," moaned Sam. But Mom stopped anyway and Linnea ran to the gate to have another look at the sign. Only half a phone number was visible.

"Looks kinda dead," said Sam who had gotten out of the car to stretch his legs.

Linnea scanned the fields with an expert eye. Four brown and black Shetlands and some Icelandic ponies grazed in the field; they looked reasonably well cared for, except for one brown one that was definitely overweight.

"I think it'll be okay here," she said, trying to sound positive. She thought with a pang about the Reingold Stables. They buzzed with activity all summer long: the little wooden cabin where the girls would sit waiting for their lessons, the tidy stable yard with its hanging baskets and cheerful red buckets, and the constant rumble of cars up and down the drive. Pia and Else must already be wondering why she hadn't come.

"It'll be okay," she repeated, trying to convince

herself. Then she looked to her right and gasped with amazement, for standing there, apart from the other horses in a field of its own, stood the most beautiful dappled gray pony she had ever seen. Tall and proud looking, it seemed to have walked out of the pages of a fairy tale. She touched the rope loop on the gate and began to walk toward it as if in a trance.

"Oh no you don't!" shouted Mom from the car. "There'll be plenty of time for ponies later on. Your brother wants to get to the house now and so do I."

Linnea reluctantly closed the gate again, but she was hardly aware of her actions. She knew that she had fallen under a spell.

"I'll be back," she whispered to the pony, "you can count on that." The pony stood still and watched her. Was it Linnea's imagination, or did the beautiful creature slightly nod its head in acknowledgement?

Max's summer house was a few yards further down the road.

"Here we are," said Mom as she coaxed the car over the bumpy driveway.

"Which part do we live in?" asked Sam. It was a good question. The house consisted of three sections: a central piece and two separate wings that jutted forwards. Normally, with houses of this design, you would expect to live in the middle section, but the windows were completely overgrown with ivy. Long grass grew across the front door, which clearly hadn't been opened in years. The left hand wing looked more promising. The pathway around it was clear and the walls looked recently painted.

"Let's try the left part first," said Mom, pulling a key from her pocket. It didn't fit the door.

"Uh-oh!" said Sam as they turned to look at the right hand wing. It seemed like the most dilapidated part of the house. A few random planks had been nailed across gaps in the original woodwork and the door boasted an eye-level square of dirty yellow glass.

"Here we go," said Mom, slipping the key into the lock. The door opened easily.

"I can't see a thing in here," said Sam. "Anybody see a light switch?" Linnea ran her hand along the wall and found one. A very weak greenish light came on and revealed their fate. Three dusty and ripped brown sofas, a pink and brown swirling linoleum floor, three different faded and peeling wallpapers, and a few cardboard boxes.

"Oh," said Mom.

"Oh," said Sam.

"Oh," said Linnea.

There isn't much more you can say when you were about to start your summer vacation in a dump. The kitchen was just as bad; ancient fitted cabinets with missing doors, a dusty, broken stove and spiders in the sink.

"Let's go upstairs," said Sam. "It can't be worse." But it was. The two bedrooms were in the attic. There was some natural light getting in through dirty dormer windows, but not much. There were no beds, a few broken chairs, and one chest of drawers.

"Thank goodness we brought the cots," said Mom with a sigh.

Sam opened the drawers listlessly. "Just old newspapers," he said, dropping them on the floor in disgust.

Linnea automatically bent down to pick them up. Tidying up after Sam was the only way to cope with living with him. She glanced at the articles, which were local news from ten years ago. Then she noticed a photo of the riding school and her eyes widened with surprise. It was the same and yet very different. The yellow farmhouse looked fresh and lived in. There was a tidy white picket fence and a newly painted sign where Linnea had earlier found a broken one.

"Tragedy at Farhult," ran the headline.

"Anything good?" asked Mom, who came over to look.

"No. Nothing," said Linnea hastily. She shoved the paper to the bottom of the pile and resolved to read it later when she was alone.

4: Riding Skills

The next morning, Linnea woke at six. There were no blinds or curtains to keep the sun from streaming in and it was too light to go back to sleep. Sam snored quietly in the other bed, curled up in a ball inside his sleeping bag.

At first Linnea decided to lie in bed and daydream. She yawned, stretched and started to consider the wallpaper. This was a more promising activity than it would have been at home. There were at least six different patterns on display and Linnea spent an idle half hour working out their order. The small sprig of blue flowers on a brownish background seemed to be the oldest since there was only a small patch of it in an awkward corner over the built-in cupboard that no one had bothered to re-paper. A frightening green swirly pattern dominated large chunks of the wall and made Linnea feel like a mermaid trapped in seaweed. This was the most recent and most disastrous choice.

Linnea selected a pale yellow paper, three layers down, as her favorite. She tried to imagine how sunny and fresh the room would look if it were all that color and decided to suggest it to Mom.

As Linnea pondered the wallpaper, she became aware of lumps in her cot; a largish mountain to the left of her foot, a ridge of small hills running under her spine and a major peak north of her head. This was backache country. She decided to get up and tackle the ladder that led to the ground floor.

"Morning Lin, couldn't you sleep any more?" asked Mom as she hovered over a battered saucepan of simmering water. "Do you know where we packed the coffee?"

"It's inside the cereal box," replied Linnea croakily. "Is there any juice?" After some rummaging they assembled a breakfast tray and shuffled out into the courtyard. Mom had made a bench from a plank and two old canisters and they sat in the sun breathing in the comforting smell of the warm wooden wall behind them.

"Can I go to the stable today?" asked Linnea after Mom had finished her first cup of coffee. She knew from experience never to ask Mom anything before the magic brown liquid had done its work.

"Yes, okay," said Mom, "have a look." Then her face clouded. "But first find out what everything costs."

Linnea nodded. She was used to this. After she had downed a final glass of juice, she put on her jeans, T-shirt and riding boots and set off down the lane. Of course no one would be riding at this time of day but she might find someone mucking out or filling up the ponies' water troughs. She could ask a few questions before everyone else arrived. It would be the perfect time of day for some light reconnaissance work.

The ponies, all hoping for apples and a little attention,

gathered at the edge of the field as she approached. All, that is, except one. The gray pony lay in the shade of a birch tree, cut off from the rest by barbed wire. She followed Linnea with her eyes but made no move to get up. Was she aloof, or defeated? Linnea couldn't decide.

"Why aren't you with the other ponies?" she asked under her breath. "Have you been naughty?" At this the gray rose quickly and stepped behind a veil of low hanging birch branches. Linnea felt a wave of regret. She wanted to get close to the pony, to stroke it and show it some tenderness, but on closer inspection she realized this would be difficult. For some reason the gray's field was completely landlocked. You could get to it only by walking through one of the other pony fields. This was impractical enough, but to make matters worse, three strands of barbed wire ran around the field without interruption and there was no gate. Linnea frowned. She had never seen a field quite like it. Who would put a pony in a field with no gate? The gray continued to ignore her so she walked back toward the lifeless yellow farmhouse.

Ahead of her was a tack shed loosely secured with a padlock. Further to her right a large trailer was stationed beside a set of rusting steps. The door was bolted and Linnea decided not to venture in. Opposite the trailer a row of ropes had been slung onto the fence at intervals, perhaps marking the different tethering places for ponies to be tacked up. Linnea was just about to have a little chat with a small black Shetland when she heard whistling coming from behind the farm. Suddenly shy, she darted behind a pile of birch logs and hid.

A slim redheaded girl rounded the corner and Linnea stifled a laugh. The girl was dressed in full cowboy gear: cowboy boots, fringed leather trousers, buckled belt, checkered shirt and a buckskin vest emblazoned with the words "Montana, Mountain Paradise."

"Howdy!" she shouted to the Shetland and she ran toward it brandishing a carrot. "See! I've brought you a treat."

The pony flicked her ears backwards in fear. Undaunted, the girl shoved the carrot under the pony's mouth and stood perilously close to the Shetland's front hoof. Linnea winced at the memory of being stepped on. She wondered how much protection the cowboy boots would afford. Next the pony sank its teeth into the carrot but the girl forgot to take her hand away. Surely some bitten fingers would result from this. But before Linnea could shout a warning, the girl took four large steps back from the pony's flank.

"Okay baby," she cried "Montana here we come!" She charged at the pony and hurled herself onto its bare back. The Shetland reared up immediately, throwing the girl to the ground. Linnea could bear it no longer. She shot out from her hiding place, grabbed the girl by the arm and heaved. Her back strained against the girl's weight but her mind was entirely focused on getting her out from under the hind hooves of the shaken Shetland pony which was still bucking and trying to break free of her tethering lead.

Once she had moved to a safe spot, Linnea slipped both arms under the girl's armpits and dragged her to a makeshift bench along the near side of the trailer. The girl felt as lifeless as a rag doll.

"Hi! Hi! Are you okay?" she cried. The girl's face was pale and her eyes looked glassy. "Please say something," pleaded Linnea. The girl's lips began to move.

"Ever been to a rodeo?" she whispered. Linnea stared.

"I said, have you ever been to a rodeo?" asked the girl again. Linnea shook her head and the girl smiled.

"They ride bareback," she said.

"I see," replied Linnea, wondering if the girl was delirious.

"But maybe I need more practice," concluded the cowgirl. She eased her legs off the bench and swung into a sitting position.

"Ohhhh," she groaned, "I feel a little weird."

"You're probably winded," explained Linnea, thinking of all the falls she had taken in her riding career. She looked closely at the girl's face, and her gaze was met by a pair of large green eyes with no fear in them. The girl smiled at Linnea and touched her shoulder.

"So what's your name? I'm Emmy. My real name is Siv but I'm going to live in Montana and herd cattle so I changed it."

"I see," said Linnea. She didn't understand why going to Montana meant you had to change your name, but it seemed too early to get bogged down in details.

"I'm Linnea," she said.

"Can you ride?" asked Emmy with a wince of pain as she straightened her back.

"Yeah," said Linnea, "it's my favorite thing."

"Me too, me too," said Emmy excitedly, "it's just that I'm no good yet. Can you help me learn? I've been taking lessons for weeks but it's not sinking in too well."

28

"I guess you need to master the basics before you try bareback," replied Linnea with a smile. Emmy nodded.

"I know, I know, it's just that they do it in Montana. I couldn't resist trying it out before the others arrive. Anyway, what were *you* doing skulking behind the woodpile?"

Linnea paused.

"Oh, good," said Emmy, "I love secrets. Spit it out. You're safe with me."

To her surprise, Linnea felt that this lousy rider, this frightener of horses, this cowgirl maniac, was entirely safe with secrets. She wasn't even sure how she knew this, she just did.

"I needed to check prices before everyone comes," she explained, "my mom's on her own so money is –"

Immediately Emmy put her hand over Linnea's mouth. "Don't say another word. I'll get a price list for you. I know where they are. But watch your back because…"

At that moment they heard voices from behind the farmhouse. A group of girls in riding gear appeared.

"Oh look!" shrieked the tallest girl. "How touching! The cowgirl has found a pet."

"She's just saved my life." Emmy declared, putting her arm around her new friend. The tall girl came to stand right in front of Linnea, closer than would normally be polite. She had a long snake-like black braid and small, dark eyes. Linnea could feel the girl's breath on her cheek. Her friends hung back, giggling nervously.

"I'm Elke," the girl said and she made it sound like a threat. Then she turned and walked back to her friends.

"I hope you don't mind," she said, without turning back, "but there's no ponies left for new riders. They've all been taken."

"That's a lie," protested Emmy. "Holly hasn't been ridden for weeks." Linnea's heart missed a beat. Which pony was Holly? Was she the beautiful gray alone in that field?

"Holly!" scoffed Elke. There were peals of laughter from Elke's fan club: a plump girl in pink rubber boots, a gaunt girl with white blond hair and a weedy-looking brunette.

"You can't exactly ride Holly!"

"Why not?" asked Linnea, goaded into speech by Elke's rudeness. "All ponies can be ridden. It's just a matter of skill."

"Oh really?" said Elke with a sneer. "Perhaps you'd like to *show* us your skill, then? Because Joanna has been riding all her life," she pointed to the large girl in the pink boots, "and so has Laura," the gaunt girl smirked, "so we're not exactly lacking in experience around here."

Linnea said nothing, but Elke was goaded now and seemed determined to make her point.

"Minette, fetch Jasper," she said, clicking her fingers. The brunette scurried off and returned with the largest Icelandic pony. He was a magnificent creature, sturdy and chestnut. Linnea's heart began to thump.

"Take Jasper around the jumps," commanded Elke, winding her long braid around her forearm. "We'll soon see what *you're* made of." Linnea hesitated.

"What's the matter? Scared or something?"

"No," protested Linnea. "It's just that... Are we allowed to?"

"Oh, save it." groaned Elke. "If you're scared then don't bother." But Linnea didn't give her time to finish. She put her foot into the stirrup and mounted. A hush descended among the girls as Linnea rode to the first jump.

"Wait!" shouted Emmy running behind her. "Have my hat." As she passed the riding hat up to Linnea she whispered, "You show that little Miss Superior a trick or two, okay?"

Linnea smiled, still wondering how she had gotten herself into this situation in the first place.

She pictured Maggie with her blue eyes and mop of gray curls and tried to imagine what she would advise.

"Pace yourself throughout the course," she imagined her saying. "Don't sacrifice control for speed."

Linnea set Jasper for the first jump. It was heaven to be riding again. The pony soared over the jump and she paced him for the second. She decided not to look back at Elke. Jasper was into his stride now and he took jump after jump with calm assurance. Linnea could feel his strength but she contained him well all the way around. She made a clean run and then cantered back to the tethering fence.

Only Emmy was waiting for her. Elke and her friends had disappeared into the tack shed.

"She's pretending she doesn't care," said Emmy with a wink, "but you really showed her."

"Minette, I need Jasper," came an imperious voice

from inside the tack shed and the dutiful brunette jogged over to get him. Once she was mounted on Jasper, Elke looked down her nose at Linnea.

"Well, we're looking forward to seeing you ride Holly, aren't we girls?" There was more tittering from her friends.

At that moment a sandy-haired woman in jodhpurs arrived and silence fell.

"I'm Ruth Summerby, the riding instructor here. I'd like to know what you were doing riding Jasper before the start of the lesson? Who are you anyway?" she barked.

Linnea gave her name and then hesitated. "I'm sorry," she began, "I didn't know."

"You're forbidden to ride here without my permission and presence. Is that understood?" continued Ruth.

Linnea nodded sheepishly. She stole a look at Elke and regretted it instantly. The girl was staring at her with venomous delight.

"Do you wish to ride here regularly?" pressed Ruth. Now Linnea felt herself go hot. She didn't dare sign up for lessons. In the excitement over Emmy's fall and Elke's challenge she had forgotten to ask about prices. What if it was too expensive?

"I would like to help out," she stammered. "Mucking out, and tacking up."

The instructor's eyes narrowed.

"As you see, we have no stabling here. The ponies stay out in summer."

"There's no shortage of muck, though," sneered Elke.

Linnea cast her eye over the fields behind her. It was true. No one seemed to care about this place. Horse muck lay decomposing everywhere, fences had been roughly patched and even the jumps were propped precariously on old logs and oil cans.

"Riders are expected to tack up for themselves," continued Ruth. "There's no work for you here." She pulled a list from her pocket and began to run through the participants for the first lesson.

"How can you say that?" protested Linnea. "There's plenty to do. The water troughs are empty, the tethering ropes are useless, and there's far too much muck in the fields."

The instructor fixed her with cold, pale eyes.

"I'm sorry if this school is not up to your exacting standards," she replied.

"That's not what I meant," stammered Linnea. She felt her neck prickling with heat and embarrassment. "I would like to ride here, but…"

"You can't afford it!" jeered Elke. Linnea looked at the ground.

Then Ruth paused and looked steadily at Linnea as if she were considering some invisible list of accounts.

"You can ride Holly," she decided. "No fee."

"You can't do that!" protested Elke.

There was a murmur of agreement from the other girls.

"Holly needs riding," said Ruth firmly. "Yes or no?"

"Thank you," Linnea replied. "I'll ride Holly.

5: Gray Mystery Investigations

Later, when Linnea thought about her day at the riding school, she realized that nothing was as it should have been. Everything was out of joint, disconnected from the true state of things. Like a riddle deliberately hiding its solution.

Mud paths, baked hard in the sun, crisscrossed the largest field and each rider led her mount carefully along the routes toward the tethering place. Linnea looked again toward the gray. No paths interrupted the immaculate green of her field.

So you're Holly, thought Linnea and she decided that Ruth would have to use wire clippers to let the beautiful creature out. Holly had all of Storm's stature and the same sense of superiority but, unlike Storm, she had a deep air of melancholy about her. Why was it that none of the other girls wanted to ride her?

Linnea pointed over to the far field.

"What's wrong with Holly, anyway? Why is she on her own like that?"

"Oh that's not Holly," replied Ruth, laughing. "Look, Elke is bringing Holly over now." Linnea's heart sank as she watched Elke approach, dragging the overweight brown Icelandic that she had noticed the previous day.

"Stubborn as an ox and fat as a barrel," declared Elke delightedly.

"Thank you," said Linnea, determined not to let Elke see her disappointment. "I'll tack her up."

It was hotter now, and Linnea began to sweat under her riding hat. The birches behind the riding tracks rustled a little in the breeze. Linnea could make out a patch of sea glittering at the foot of the escarpment. After months in the city it was a welcome sight. She wondered where the nearest swimming place was and laughed at herself for not having asked Max such a crucial question. She buckled Holly's saddle, trying not to notice its dilapidated state.

The lesson got underway and Linnea struggled. Holly walked as though she were wading through mud and wouldn't trot at all. It was all Linnea could do to get her to turn left or right, and she wasn't always successful even at that. The pony seemed to have a mind of its own and only occasionally did what it was told, just to keep the peace.

"Great riding skills!" laughed Elke as Holly once again abandoned the exercises and started grazing absentmindedly in the middle of the circle. Linnea felt utterly helpless on this hopeless pony.

Emmy was struggling too. It was no wonder that she had been finding it hard to make progress, Linnea thought. In a normal riding school she would be in a proper beginners class but here the small numbers meant that everyone was thrown in together. A couple of boys arrived late and seemed reluctant to learn anything. They rode badly and spent as much time as possible joshing each other and sharing private jokes. After an hour Linnea was desperate for the end.

"Okay, that's it for now," said Ruth at last. "Make your way to the tethering fence. We'll try some of these exercises again on Wednesday."

Emmy and Linnea tethered their ponies side by side.

"You're really good," said Emmy enviously, "I wish I could ride like you."

"Don't be crazy," sighed Linnea. "I was useless."

"You haven't seen the others on Holly!" laughed Emmy. "Last week Joanna spent the whole lesson trying to get her to stand up. That pony should be shot!"

Linnea turned on Emmy.

"Never say that!" she shouted. "Never, ever say that!"

Emmy blushed. "I'm sorry," she said, "I didn't mean…" She couldn't finish her sentence because Ruth interrupted.

"You did okay today, Linnea," she said, "I hope you're not going to give up now." Giving up was exactly what Linnea had in mind. She wasn't sure she could stand being jeered at by Elke again.

"Can I ride that pony over there next time?" she asked, pointing over to the gray who was standing at the near side of her field as if she knew she was being discussed. Ruth laughed.

"Oh no!" she said. "No one ever rides that pony."

"Why not?" asked Linnea.

"I honestly don't know," laughed Ruth again. "I suppose it belongs to the family."

"Which family?" asked Linnea, burning with curiosity.

"The family who own this place," replied Ruth.

"Well, can I ask them permission, then?" Linnea asked. A flicker of irritation crossed Ruth's face.

"They don't live here anymore and they never come here, either, so I think that would be tricky, don't you?" She smiled but it was a brisk and business-like smile calculated to bring the conversation to a close.

"What's its name?" Linnea asked, knowing that she was overstepping her boundaries but powerless to stop herself.

"It has no name," said Ruth frowning. She whistled for her dog and strode away toward her car. "Don't be late tomorrow," she called over her shoulder, "or I'll charge you for the lesson."

Most of the girls had drifted off toward the cars that were waiting for them by the side of the road beyond the main field. There didn't seem to be much traffic on this road. A few of the mothers had gotten out of their cars to chat and pass the time until their children were ready to be taken home. Linnea watched Elke climb into a large black Mercedes SUV with darkened windows. The car set off as soon as she was inside and drove at breakneck speed along the road that led down to the coast toward the main part of the village.

Emmy was also headed for the road but she had biked.

Linnea found the sight of Emmy's flimsy old bike strangely comforting. It had been decorated in an enthusiastic style that was utterly lacking in cool. The white plastic basket attached to the handlebars was covered with large plastic flowers, most of which had lost their petals. The mudguards had little rainbows painted on them and the main chassis of the bike was covered in touring stickers suggesting untold adventures on the open road. Emmy mounted, rode a few yards and then keeled over onto the edge of the road. Linnea sprinted toward her but slowed to a jog when she realized that Emmy was doubled-up with laughter.

"That *always* happens!" she giggled. "Please don't rescue me again. This is getting embarrassing!"

Linnea helped Emmy untangle her cowgirl tassels from the spokes of her front wheel. Once she was free, they lay on the grass laughing and looking up into the sky. Neither was in a hurry to go home.

"Isn't it weird that no one rides the gray pony?" said Linnea.

"Positively spooky, if you ask me," said Emmy propping herself up on her elbows. "I think Ruth knows more about it than she's saying."

Linnea sat up suddenly. "What makes you say that?" she asked.

Emmy didn't answer right away. She started making little braids so Linnea couldn't see her face properly. Then she brushed her hair back in one brisk move and said, "It has to do with the family who owns the riding school and never go there. They paid Ruth silence money, to shut her up. I just know it."

At first Linnea thought that this was overly dramatic, but then she remembered the newspaper article about the tragedy at Farhult. Maybe there really was something that needed to be hushed up.

"A tragedy happened here many years ago. I read it in the paper," began Linnea. Emmy sat up.

"Are you serious?"

"Absolutely," said Linnea, nodding her head. "I've hidden the article back at our summer house. I'll show you if you like!"

Emmy leaped to her feet. "Come on," she said, "let's go."

"Not so fast," said Linnea. "If Mom finds out there's something weird about the riding school she'll stop me from riding there."

"All investigations will be conducted according to the strictest G.M.I. guidelines," said Emmy.

"G.M.I?" asked Linnea.

"Gray Mystery Investigations," replied Emmy. "Now, are we going to get to the bottom of this or aren't we?"

"Sure we are," said Linnea, smiling.

6: The Swim

Emmy took one look at Max's summer house and whistled.

"Kind of a mess, isn't it?" said Linnea.

"A mess, yes," said Emmy, "but it's kind of cool too. Can we go in?"

"Course," said Linnea as she opened the front door. Not much had changed since she left. Mom had cleared the breakfast table and Sam had set up his synthesizer in the downstairs room. There was a note under an old brick in the middle of the kitchen floor. "Gone to village for food and quick swim. Back one o'clock." Linnea looked at her watch. It was only eleven.

"Good," she said, "that gives us plenty of time. Follow me." She scrambled up the ladder to the second floor with Emmy right behind her.

"The article is up here," she explained. But when they checked the bedrooms there was no sign of the pile of newspapers that Linnea distinctly remembered from the previous day.

"Maybe your mom pitched them already?" suggested Emmy.

Linnea sighed. That seemed likely.

"Okay, we'll just have to check the trashcans," said Emmy. The two girls hurried downstairs again. First they investigated the bag in the kitchen that Mom was using for compost waste.

"Eww," protested Emmy as she ran her hands through soggy coffee grounds. From the shape of the bag Linnea could see that the big pile of newspapers was not inside.

"She must have put them right outside," she said.

"Your turn," said Emmy when they got there. "There might be something gross in there." But there wasn't. There was nothing in the trashcan but a stubby paintbrush covered in apple green paint, the color of Sam's bedroom before he went through his Star Wars phase.

"That's strange," said Linnea, "I didn't notice any fresh paint in the house, did you?"

"No," said Emmy turning around, "but someone's been painting that bench."

Mom's homemade courtyard bench was still dripping with green and the old newspapers were laid beneath it. Linnea closed her eyes in disbelief.

"Come on," said Emmy. "It's got to be down there somewhere." They knelt down and started coaxing the newspapers from under the bench. This was difficult since the sheets were stuck together with globs of paint. Once each piece had been rescued Emmy spread it out while Linnea rushed around the courtyard looking for stones to weigh the paper down. The sheets under the oil cans were particularly hard to move.

"Don't rush it," pleaded Linnea as she tilted the heavy can

on its side. Eventually, after twenty minutes of painstaking work, all the newspapers were laid out to dry.

"We can read the top sides first," suggested Linnea. "They'll be dry enough to turn over in half an hour." So the girls lay on their bellies in the sun and read. Local weddings, cafe openings, film reviews, council meetings, lost dogs and stolen cars; nothing escaped their notice, but there was no sign of the Farhult tragedy.

Linnea checked her watch.

"I don't know if we're going to make it," she said, "Mom and Sam are due back soon."

Five minutes later Emmy shrieked, "Come over here!"

Linnea ran to her side.

"That one?" she asked. Emmy nodded glumly. A large splotch of paint had fallen in the worst possible spot. "Tragedy at Farhult," ran the headline and the rest was a lake of green.

At that moment Mom and Sam arrived.

"Why have you moved all my stuff?" asked Sam.

"Why did you waste all this paint on a plank bench?" countered Linnea.

"There's plenty more paint," said Mom. "Who's your new friend?"

"This is Emmy from the riding club," Linnea explained.

"Pleased to meet you," said Emmy politely and without a hint of shyness.

Mom paused and considered the girl for a moment. Then she said, "So, Emmy-from-the-riding-club, will you stay for lunch?"

"Thanks," said Emmy, "as long as I don't have to sit on the bench." Everybody laughed. Sam dragged the newspaper back to his painting area, while Mom made sandwiches and the girls grabbed furniture from inside the house to make a new seating area in the shade of the largest apple tree.

"I like this place," said Emmy looking out onto the cornfield opposite. "It's poetic."

"You should try living here," protested Linnea.

"Also poetic," said Mom as she passed around a plate of rolls. "Poets should suffer for their art."

"Yeah, come and stay," said Sam. "You'll suffer, all right!"

"Be quiet, Sam," said Linnea, suddenly embarrassed.

"I live with my grandfather," said Emmy. "He's a painter."

"Is that where you got the idea for your bike?" asked Sam, and everybody started laughing again.

"How long has he lived here?" asked Linnea. She wondered if Emmy's grandfather might remember the tragedy at Farhult. Emmy smiled knowingly at her.

"We moved here last year," she said. "But, if you want to know anything about Farhult, ask Mrs. Stenson."

"The shop lady?" Mom asked.

"Yes," said Emmy. "She knows everything."

"Does she have spooky mystic powers?" asked Sam.

"Course not Sam, she's just nosy," said Mom, rolling her eyes. "Anyway, what do you want to know about Farhult, sweetheart?"

"Oh I just wanted to ask about swimming places," she said quickly. "I want to go for a swim this afternoon."

"I know all about that," said Sam proudly. "Mom and I went for a swim this morning."

"I'll take you to my secret place," promised Emmy. "Can we go when we've finished lunch, Mrs...."

"Karlsson," said Mom, "but for goodness sake, call me Karin. And yes you can."

After they finished eating the girls set off for the village with two of Linnea's swimsuits and a couple of towels stuffed into Emmy's bike basket. There was a companionable silence between them. Although Linnea could think of plenty of things she wanted to know about Emmy, she decided not to ask any questions. It was unusual to live with your grandfather, but she decided to wait for Emmy to explain. Linnea thought how glad she was that Emmy hadn't asked her about Dad. She hated it when people asked.

The ponies at the riding school ignored the girls as they walked past, and although Linnea inwardly saluted the beautiful, lonely, gray, her mind focused on the afternoon's activities and on how to extract information from Mrs. Stenson. The road dropped toward the coast and revealed more houses. Everyone seemed to have neat yards: flower beds, vegetable patches, tables for outdoor meals, barbecue corners, swings and slides and even an occasional trampoline. Linnea thought of Max's place and vowed that she would never let Mom tidy the garden. Emmy was right; it was poetic the way it was.

The road now swung left past the church and down into the harbor. The houses here were older, former fishermen's cottages with wooden picket fences and laundry hung out to dry. Linnea took a deep breath and filled her lungs with sea air. Suddenly all she could think about was a swim and she didn't care about any secret swimming hole. Families dotted the small beach to the left of the harbor wall and children played in the shallows. Linnea ran onto the sand and changed into her swimsuit. She glanced over her shoulder, but Emmy had propped her bike against a fence and was crouched down by her back wheel, so Linnea scampered into the sea as eagerly as a five-year-old.

She swam as soon as the water reached the top of her thighs and felt like a water sprite wrapped in green. She floated on her back and began to daydream. She imagined riding down the beach on the back of the beautiful gray pony, the wind blowing through her hair. They could travel south together, stopping only to grill sausages on little rock hearths. Linnea looked up into the clear blue sky and wondered whether the beautiful pony had ever been allowed to swim. They could come down to the sea at sunset when the sky was pink and the water opal. The more she thought about the pony, the more excited she felt. This would be a great vacation, she decided, maybe the best ever.

She stood up to wave to Emmy. But Emmy's bike was not there and neither was Emmy.

7: Moonlight

"I don't know much about the riding school," replied Mrs. Stenson as she put the lettuce in a plastic bag. "Neither of my boys was interested in horses. They preferred sailing. My husband runs classes from the harbor. Why don't you and your brother sign up?"

"H-H-How do you know I have a brother?" stammered Linnea.

"Came in here with your mom this morning," she replied putting her hand out for Linnea's change. Mrs. Stenson's eyes were small and lizard-like. Linnea groped in her pockets for money but failed to find any. A wiry gray-haired man in faded blue overalls stood behind her in line. Interview time was running out.

"Has Ruth always been the instructor up there?" continued Linnea trying to sound casual as she realized that she had no money for the lettuce.

"Oh, no," replied Mrs. Stenson, "Ruth's only had the job for a year or two. Doesn't cut it as an instructor though, does she?" Linnea shuffled awkwardly and avoided Mrs. Stenson's gaze.

"No, I thought not," continued the shopkeeper.

"She's an office type, actually. Works as a bookkeeper in Hemmerby. I think she just works there for the money and I don't suppose there's much of that."

"So they had a better instructor before?" asked Linnea.

"Yes," said Mrs. Stenson, "much better. The lettuce is two dollars." She waggled her outstretched hand.

Linnea took a deep breath.

"Oh dear," she said, "I think my money fell out of my pocket at the beach."

Mrs. Stenson shook her head wearily.

"Kids!" she said.

"Here, I'll pay," said the old man behind Linnea.

"Oh thank you," stammered Linnea. She couldn't ask any more questions. The man had been waiting long enough. Grabbing her lettuce, she ran out of the shop with Mrs. Stenson's beady eyes burning a hole in her back. Emmy was standing outside kicking gravel around.

"Why did you disappear like that?" asked Linnea.

"Because you annoyed me," Emmy replied.

"I did?" asked Linnea.

"Yes," said Emmy. She went into the shop and slammed the door behind her.

Linnea sat on a small wooden bench outside the shop and hugged her lettuce. A list of woes bubbled up in her mind. The cottage was awful and so was the riding school, and Emmy, who had seemed fun, was turning out to be moody. Her investigations of the gray pony had so far failed. The old man came out of the shop and Linnea gave him a grateful wave. Then she sank back into gloom. Nothing was right. Nothing. She squeezed some water out of her damp hair and set off up the hill.

She paused as she neared the riding school and glanced at her watch. It was twelve-thirty. Most people would be having lunch. She walked through the first field and assessed the barbed wire around the gray pony. It was the best stretch of fencing in the whole school; too high to climb over and too close together to scramble through. She plucked the top wire but it was taut.

"Why don't you come over and say hello?" she suggested, but the pony made no move.

"I'm not going to ignore you like everyone else," continued Linnea, "so you'd better get used to the attention." Still the pony did not move.

"Do you have a big, spooky, skeleton in your closet?" she asked, but the pony looked over Linnea's shoulder, lost in some reverie.

"Okay," said Linnea. "Be like that." Then she slithered under the wire into the field. Now the pony towered over her and Linnea felt vulnerable.

"I don't know what you've done in the past," she said, trying to keep her voice level, "but you can always start again." The pony took a tentative step toward her. She held out her hand and the pony stepped closer. There was now only a yard between them.

"You've got to trust me," said Linnea quietly. "You've got to take a chance."

The pony shuddered slightly and then nuzzled Linnea's hand. Linnea stroked its face over and over again. The animal, so long untouched, seemed to go into a trance. Then, moving cautiously, Linnea began to stroke the pony's dappled flank. There was no doubting the animal's power. Linnea made a quick mental comparison with Storm and decided that the gray's configuration was better. What would it feel like to ride her? Like magic, like flying, like being an Arabian Princess.

"I'm going to call you Moonlight," she whispered. "What do you think?" The pony snorted gently, as if she were humoring a private joke.

Have you ever ridden bareback? Suddenly Emmy's question floated into her mind. The answer was no, but now the thought was in Linnea's mind, buzzing around like an excited bee. She could ride this pony here and now. It would be so simple. *You are absolutely forbidden to ride here without my presence and permission*, Ruth had said. It would be a big risk. If Ruth caught her riding unsupervised for a second time, Linnea felt sure she would be banned from the school forever.

Linnea looked around her. There was absolutely nobody around. The farmhouse was dead as usual and the other ponies were mostly lying down. She decided not to think too much as thinking might lead to inaction. This was a day for risk. So she took a handful of the pony's forelock and pulled firmly. To her surprise, it responded.

She knows what's in my mind, she thought as she ran her hand along the pony's spine. Seizing the mane in both hands, she hauled herself onto the pony's back. Then she lay still for a few minutes, clinging like a barnacle on an upturned boat. Moonlight stood calmly with her head erect. After a few moments Linnea felt safe enough to lever herself into a sitting position.

"Okay, girl," she said, "I think I'm ready." She squeezed her heels and the pony set off.

I wish we could trot or canter, thought Linnea, but it seemed risky without a riding hat. She went around and around in circles and was struck again by Moonlight's ceremonial style. She walked as if every step counted. Linnea forgot all her frustrations with Storm and Holly. Only Moonlight mattered now. What was her past? Why had this poised and beautiful creature been ignored and imprisoned?

As she rode, Linnea suddenly noticed a corner of pink in the trees that looked like a shed or a playhouse. She realized that it could only be seen from horseback in this forbidden field, as its roofline lay below the escarpment toward the sea. She shaded her eyes and squinted in the direction of the woods. It was definitely worth investigating.

She dismounted and put her hands on either side of Moonlight's neck.

"Don't worry. I'll be back," she whispered. Then she slithered under the barbed wire and walked toward the escarpment. When she glanced back Moonlight was watching her, waiting for her to return.

Linnea reached an area of low scrub and sapling birches. There were no paths so she clambered over fallen branches and through patches of creeping blueberry until she reached the small pink structure. It had seen better days. Close up, the shed was so weather-beaten that it no longer looked pink, but as Linnea ran her hand over the rough wood she could see shards of rose-colored paint in its fissures. The door was padlocked so she walked around the shed looking for a window. There was none. She tried to peep between the planks of wood, but this didn't work either. Frustrated, she kicked the bottom of the shed. Then she noticed a small peephole where a knot had fallen out of a plank. By putting her eye up close to the hole, she could see the floor of the shed.

A book lay open on a gray rag rug, its yellowing pages splayed out. There was also a pair of cherry red party shoes. *About my size*, thought Linnea as she sat up again. So this *was* a playhouse, but whose? And when was it abandoned? How long would it take for a book to turn yellow like that? Five or ten years? If the girl who used the playhouse had been thirteen at the time she would be eighteen or twenty-three by now. Linnea shuddered. A cool breeze blew up from the coast below.

She paced once more around the playhouse. *I have to get in there*, she thought. She ran her hand along a length of plank and mentally inserted a long screwdriver behind it. Maybe it would give. The best way to get inside would be to coax two planks off the shed's frame. Then she could climb in and out easily. If she nailed the planks back afterwards no one would know she had been there. *It's not really breaking in*, she thought.

Linnea walked back toward the main road with her head full of plans. As she drew level with the farmhouse a squirrel darted across her path. Linnea watched it climb up the tree stump by the back door. Then she saw it. A hand twitched a curtain from inside the farmhouse. It was a slim, fragile hand.

Terrified, Linnea ran. Through the fields, along the road, up, up, until she reached the summer house. Her heart banged and her throat rasped but she didn't care. Still trembling, she threw herself onto the cool grass of the orchard like an exhausted dog.

8: A Red Sports Car

"So when's he coming?" asked Sam eagerly.

"This weekend. Apparently he wants to assess the damage," replied Mom. She didn't sound bothered, which immediately awakened Linnea's suspicions.

"Cool," said Sam. "We can go and kick a ball together."

Mom was setting the table in the courtyard for supper. She paused for a moment and looked concerned.

"Sam, honey, I don't know if he'll want to …"

She didn't finish the sentence. Sam kicked a spray of stones angrily toward the table and then skidded into the house. There was an awkward silence. Then Mom said, "Linnea, can *you* talk to him?"

Linnea bit her lip. There was no right way to handle Sam during these moments; you just had to wait for them to pass. Mom always thought that someone should talk to him, but talking usually made it worse. Sam longed for his dad. So did Linnea. She struggled to push thoughts of Dad out of her mind; the last morning when he had kissed her on the forehead as he always did, and Mom's torrents of tears when the news had come and the long weeks afterwards when nobody knew what to say. Linnea steered the conversation back to Max's visit.

"So how long is he staying?"

"Just Friday, Saturday and Sunday night," said Mom as she laid out the glasses.

A three night stay to check over a ruined summer house? Linnea smiled to herself.

"That's great, Mom," she said simply. Mom looked flustered.

"Stop looking at me like that," she said.

"Like what?" asked Linnea, innocently.

"Like that," said Mom, and she hurried back into the kitchen.

Later they sat together in the courtyard dipping strawberries into a pot of whipped cream.

"You're hogging it," protested Sam.

"I thought you didn't like cream," replied Linnea airily.

"Yeah, well I do now," said Sam.

"Oh Linnea," said Mom who was sipping more coffee, "that friend of yours dropped by again this afternoon."

"Emmy?"

"Yes. She came into the house with a note for you. Said she couldn't find our mailbox. I put it on your bed."

"Can I get it now?" asked Linnea. Usually Mom didn't let children get up from table in the middle of a meal. It was one of her "things," but this time she nodded, so Linnea ran into the house licking cream off her fingers as she went.

A small silver envelope lay on her bed. It was bulging.

Linnea ripped it open and white rose petals tumbled out. There was also a small sheet of blue paper. Emmy's handwriting was bold and curvaceous. *I was really angry when you just jumped into the sea and didn't wait for me to show you my special place. But the rose is for forgiveness. Next time you have to come to my secret bathing spot or else!* Ah! So that had been the problem. *Mrs. T. Johnston is the key to all knowledge,* continued the letter. *She was the last riding instructor at Farhult and worked there for twenty years. She lives in Hemmerby and I've got her address. See you behind the woodpile at dawn. No. Just kidding. Be at the lesson tomorrow for next meting of the G.M.I.* The note was signed *Emilia-Maria Von Richtershausen*.

Very posh thought Linnea, *but you've already told me your name's Siv.*

The next morning Linnea set off early for the riding school. Of course the riding would be disappointing, she knew that now, but at least she and Emmy had something to work on. They could discuss the playhouse, and there was also the important matter of how to interview Mrs. Johnston. But when Linnea reached the main gate she was disappointed to find that Emmy's bike was not there. She marched briskly to the tack shed wondering if her unpredictable friend would be hiding behind the woodpile. Instead she walked straight into Elke.

"Watch where you're going!" Elke shouted, glowering.

"I'm sorry," stammered Linnea, "I didn't see you there."

"Why do you bother coming anyway?" asked Elke with a flick of her ponytail. "It's perfectly obvious you can't ride."

Linnea pretended to ignore her.

"You'll never learn anything coming here like this. Shame you haven't got your own pony. If you buy one you might improve enough to ride here next year," continued Elke. "But if I rode as badly as you I'd probably just give up."

"I see," said Linnea, trying to control her desire to push Elke into the dust. "So how long have you been riding?"

"All my life," replied the girl, "so I know a hopeless case when I see one."

Linnea took a deep breath and thrust her hands into her pockets.

"What about the gray over there?" she asked. "Is that pony a hopeless case as well?"

"Depends on if you want a broken neck," said Elke with a malicious smile, and then she glided off to the tack shed with her nose in the air.

To Linnea's irritation, Emmy was late for the class so there was no chance to talk. Ruth followed the same routine she had used for the previous lesson. Around and around the track they rode repeating the same old exercises. Linnea thought about Maggie's lessons at Reingold. She always made the lessons fun and unpredictable. One day she had made all the girls ride in a circle sitting on their hands! Else and Pia had nearly died laughing, but they had managed it. "Nothing matters

more than your feel for the pony," Maggie would say.
"I'm just trying to get you to relax with each other."
Ruth seemed to have a very different aim. She barked
instructions like a sergeant major on a parade ground.

"Tuck your knees in, Laura. Minette, stop chatting.
Joanna, you're sitting like a sack of potatoes."

The overall effect was not helpful. It was just
annoying. Like being caught in a rainstorm. With one
or two gentle words Maggie could teach someone more
about riding than this woman ever could.

Emmy struggled on but it was not a pretty sight. She
held the reins too slack and leaned too far forward. It
was a miracle she stayed on at all during the trotting.
Elke and her friends seemed to survive by ignoring
Ruth completely. From time to time Elke gave the
instructor a supercilious stare and disobeyed her
instructions completely. To Linnea's surprise Ruth
did not challenge Elke's behavior. Instead she would
suddenly find something urgent to do which prevented
her from noticing. She'd fiddle with her whip or switch
her attention to one of the other riders. It was all very
strange. Linnea was relieved when the lesson ended; she
dismounted and led Holly back to the tethering place.
She was desperate to speak to Emmy but also very aware
that Elke's eyes followed her mercilessly, almost as if she
suspected something.

"Walk home with me," she muttered to Emmy. "Can't
speak now." Emmy nodded and then ignored Linnea
so completely that no one would have guessed they
were friends. Linnea started to walk home, and a full

five minutes later Emmy clunked up behind her on her dilapidated bike.

"So, did you get my letter?"

"Yeah. Of course. But how are we going to get to Hemmerby to interview that woman?"

"Dunno," said Emmy. "I thought you might have an idea."

Linnea didn't, but she told Emmy about the abandoned playhouse.

"Emmy, there was another thing. I saw a hand moving a curtain inside the farmhouse."

"No way!" said Emmy. She stopped in her tracks and whistled. "Are you sure?"

"Yes," said Linnea. "I thought the farmhouse was deserted; otherwise I wouldn't have risked snooping around. It was the last thing I expected." A small sparrow landed on the road a few feet in front of the girls. He looked quizzically at them, twisting his head from side to side. *So what are you going to do about it?* he seemed to be asking.

"That is super spooky," said Emmy with a shiver. "Maybe someone's being held hostage there or something. What size hand was it?"

"Woman or child," replied Linnea.

Emmy looked at the ground thoughtfully.

"We're definitely onto something now. Gray Mystery Investigations has two leads to follow. Playhouse *and* farmhouse."

When they reached the summer house a shiny red Alpha Romeo sports car was parked outside.

"Nice car," said Emmy, "That yours?"

"No," replied Linnea, puzzled. "I don't know whose it is."

At that moment the front door banged open and Sam charged out in his soccer gear.

"See you!" he called and ran down the road into the village. Next came Max O'Leary in shorts. His sneakers were ancient and spattered with paint and he wore a hooded college soccer jersey, which suggested some sort of team membership, but most of the words had peeled off.

"Don't laugh," he ordered. "I'm going to play 'footie' with Sam. If I don't come back, tell my mother I loved her," and he ran after Sam with a lolloping gait.

Linnea grabbed Emmy's hand and ran into the house to find Mom singing at the sink. She stopped as soon as the girls arrived.

"What's he doing here?" asked Linnea.

"He came to check the house," replied Mom.

"Yeah, but this isn't the weekend."

"No, it isn't," agreed Mom.

"But you said he was coming this weekend."

"Yes, I suppose he changed his mind," said Mom.

"So he's come four days early?" continued Linnea incredulously.

"Yes."

"How long is he staying?"

"I don't know." Mom replied, looking embarrassed, "I haven't asked him."

"What do you mean you haven't asked him?" Linnea

continued. She had never heard anything so unlikely in her whole life. Mom was the most organized person she knew.

"Well, I think it's wonderful that he's come," said Emmy, nudging Linnea to be quiet. "I'm sure he's a very nice person and it's our job to make him feel welcome. There's a famous coffee house in Hemmerby and I suggest we take him there for lunch."

Linnea groaned inwardly. Mom didn't have the money to take everyone out to lunch.

"What a good idea," said Mom sweetly. "Emmy, give your grandfather a quick call to see if you can come. Tell him you'll be back by five o'clock."

9: Hemmerby at Last

The coffee house was a low-ceilinged log cabin. It would have been cozy in the winter, but today it was uncomfortably hot. There were only a few elderly couples having quiet cups of coffee and the waitress looked irritated and bored. Sam demanded to sit next to Max at lunch and bombarded him with chatter. Max chatted back good-naturedly but Linnea could see that it was making Mom uneasy. Eventually Mom told Sam to quiet down and he sulked for the rest of the meal.

Linnea and Emmy drained huge glasses of cola and then spent the rest of the meal getting up to use the toilet, which exasperated Mom. She kept apologizing to Max as if everything had to be perfect and she seemed not to be able to think of anything else to say. And Max, usually so easygoing, also looked inhibited. When they finished desert, Mom suggested returning to Farhult. She looked tense and unhappy. Lunch had not been a success. Emmy and Linnea exchanged glances. The chance to find Mrs. Johnston seemed to be slipping away.

"I know," said Linnea suddenly. "Why don't we split up? We kids can go down to the harbor and watch the boats for a while and you two can have a quiet chat?" To her relief, Mom and Max agreed willingly.

The harbor was bustling with activity. Yachts and fishing boats bobbed up and down on their moorings and a few boys were diving off the harbor wall and into the deep, cold sea. Toddlers lay on their bellies on the wooden jetty with rudimentary fishing lines made of clothes pegs and string, waiting for crabs to take their bait. Seagulls flew overhead. For a moment Linnea was transported to the long summers of her earliest memories. She was a little kid again, and she needed nothing more in life than a bucket, a spade and some gooey seaweed with which to frighten Sam.

Sam was also contented. He sat on the harbor wall dangling his legs and giggled at a couple of eight-year-old boys struggling to get a steep-sided sailing boat out to sea. Only Emmy seemed restless.

"How are we going to get away?" she muttered constantly to Linnea. "We've got to go soon or we'll miss our chance. What if her place is closed in the afternoon?"

Reluctantly Linnea agreed.

"Sam, we're going to the stores. Wanna come?" she asked. Sam loathed shopping and didn't bother replying.

Linnea and Emmy headed to the main shopping area where Mrs. Johnston had her practice. Bunting was draped across the street to give the town a vacation-feel, but in truth Hemmerby had little to offer. The only clothes shop displayed flowery swimsuits for plump ladies, and the toyshop had gone under. The small supermarket was fairly busy, but the magazine stand had shut for lunch and not bothered to reopen. They found Tilda Johnston's practice between the optician's and a hardware store.

"What are we going to do when we get in there?" asked Linnea, suddenly panicking.

"Dunno," said Emmy, "you'll think of something," and she pushed Linnea through the door. A few magazines and some black leather chairs suggested that this was a waiting room although there was no receptionist. A door paned with frosted glass led off to the right and Linnea could hear voices behind it.

Emmy curled up in one of the leather chairs and started flicking through "Star Gossip."

"I want to catch up on who's dating who," she explained.

"Oh great," said Linnea. "So I have to do a tricky interview while you read Hollywood mags."

"Yup," replied Emmy and Linnea had to resist a strong urge to kick her. At that moment a head poked out of the treatment room.

"I'm sorry, do you have an appointment?" The expression on the woman's face showed that she knew they didn't.

"Are you Mrs. Johnston?" stammered Linnea, playing for time.

"Yes," she replied, "If you want an appointment you'll have to call or come back tomorrow morning when my receptionist is here."

"We can't come back tomorrow," said Emmy coolly from behind her magazine. "By the way, do you think that Christina D'Arcy really *is* in love with Robbie Markham?" The physiotherapist raised her eyebrows with irritation.

"I have no idea," she said briskly. "I have to get back to my patient. Please come back another time."

"It's just that Christina is *so* beautiful and Robbie Markham is *so* old," continued Emmy.

"We urgently need an appointment for my dad," said Linnea quickly. "He hurt his back so badly that he can't get out of bed. We must have an appointment for this evening because he's giving a lecture tomorrow at the University."

"What, during summer vacation?" asked the physiotherapist sounding unconvinced.

"Last week of term," piped up Emmy again. "They have different vacations there."

"I see," said Mrs. Johnston. She seemed impressed. Linnea guessed that, living in this sleepy seaside town, Tilda Johnston didn't often get the chance to rescue incapacitated vacationing lecturers.

"Where are you staying?" she asked.

"Farhult, 32 Main Street," replied Linnea quick as a flash.

"That's on my way home," said Tilda, "I could stop by at five? It can't be much later as I'm picking up my son from his friend's at six."

"Perfect" said Emmy, jumping to her feet. "We'll be expecting you."

The physiotherapist disappeared back into her treatment room and the two girls dashed out of the waiting room onto the street where they collapsed into fits of giggles.

"I can't believe we just did that," gasped Linnea. "What were you doing babbling on about movie stars?"

"All I could think of at the time," laughed Emmy. "Anyway, I knew you'd come up with something."

"Well I came up with total nonsense. Where am I going to get a bedridden father from?"

There was an awkward pause. Emmy played with the catch on her belt.

"You haven't mentioned your dad before," she said quietly.

"No," said Linnea. "I don't have one anymore."

To Linnea's relief Emmy asked nothing more and they wandered back to the harbor.

She would have to ask Max to fake a bad back. But would he listen to the mystery of the gray pony and go along with the ploy? She thought he probably would. Why was it that you instinctively trusted some people and not others? Why could a pony be calm with some riders and wild with others? What were the invisible threads between people and animals which made them grow closer together or drift further apart? Linnea felt it had something to do with risk. Every time you met a person or an animal you took a little risk. You held out your hand and waited. She thought how Max had taken a chance with her and Sam on that first evening in the apartment. He'd offered his summer house to a pair of kids he'd never met before. And he had asked them to persuade Mom. That was the gist of the risk, she realized now, to make it obvious that he liked Mom.

Mom and Max were waiting in the parking lot as agreed. They were sitting perched on the hood of the car with their feet on the bumper. Mom was wearing a lime green shirt, knotted at the waist, and she was laughing at some story Max was telling her. Linnea thought how young and carefree she looked and realized with a shock that this was how Mom always used to look. She had a sudden, overwhelming desire to lead Emmy and Sam back to the harbor, to the supermarket or even to the closed toyshop so that they wouldn't interrupt. But it was too late. Max saw them and jumped off the hood.

10: Red Pajamas

"Well this is the strangest lumbar injury I've ever come across," said Tilda as she rubbed some more gel onto Max's back.

"Yeah, I find it pretty surprising myself," said Max with an entirely straight face. At this point Emmy staggered out of the room, no longer able to contain herself. Linnea buried her face in her hands for at least the third time and tried to think about something sad to keep from laughing. Max was playing his part too well.

"My problem, Tilda, is that I'm physically inactive. If I did more exercise like my um, daughter Linnea here, then these kinds of injuries wouldn't happen, would they?"

"That's right," agreed Tilda, "Your muscle tone is poor."

"I thought I might take up horseback riding," continued Max, who then winked shamelessly at Linnea, "Can you recommend anywhere locally?"

"There's a riding school next door!" exclaimed Tilda. "Haven't you noticed?"

"Well of course," protested Max, "but it seems pretty run down to me."

"It's fine for beginners," said Tilda as she rolled up her sleeves. "I used to be the instructor there. Now roll onto your side and sit on the edge of the bed, please."

"So, who owns that school?" asked Max. He winced as Tilda started pummeling his back.

"Eva Malmgren," said Tilda. Her face was becoming red with exertion.

"The farmland was sold ten years ago, but Eva kept the riding school and the house."

Linnea's mind started to whirr. Ten years ago, the time of the tragedy. Had it ruined the family farm too?

"So what happened?" Max asked. "Why did Eva sell the land?"

"I don't think we need to go into that now," said Tilda guardedly.

"Go into what?" asked Linnea politely.

"Water under the bridge." said Tilda firmly. "We don't talk about those things any more."

There was an awkward silence. Then Linnea took a deep breath and decided to go for it.

"Look," she said, "there's a beautiful gray pony that no one rides. It's in a field all on its own surrounded by barbed wire. No animal should be treated like that. I need to see this Eva Malmgren and talk to her about it."

Tilda rubbed some more gel onto her hands.

"You people are new to this area, so I am going to give you a tip, okay? Leave Eva Malmgren alone. What's happened has happened. There's nothing anyone can do about it now. So go to her riding school if you want to ride, but leave the poor woman in peace."

"Linnea didn't mean to intrude," said Max defensively. "As you say, we're new to the area. Off you go, Linnea," he said gently. "Go and find Emmy." Linnea left the room, grateful to get away.

Forty-five minutes later Mom and Sam returned from their swim. Sam, who had agreed to get Mom out of the way, was now eager to claim his reward, and reluctantly Linnea followed him out to the soccer field. Emmy had gone home for supper with her grandfather. They had only chatted briefly about Tilda.

"At least we now know about Eva Malmgren." Emmy had said. "She's the key to everything."

Emmy was right. The investigation had advanced. Now they knew the name of the riding school owner. It was a good start. Linnea felt her spirits rise as they reached the soccer field, fringed with tall silver birch trees. A small boy and his sister were sitting together in the sand, making an elaborate mud pie. Beyond the swings two old men were playing a leisurely game of tennis. The steady plock, plock, plock of the ball being hit was, to Linnea's ears, the perfect summery sound. The sun had begun to sink but the sky was still blue and the evening light was warm and golden.

She stood in the goal and decided to concentrate on the ball. Sam had been a star. This was the least she could do to repay him.

"So why did I have to get Mom out of the way?" asked Sam once he was into his stride with his shots. Linnea smiled to herself. She thought of all the conversations she had had with her brother while balls flew at her face. It felt normal. So normal in fact that she couldn't imagine how they would talk about anything if Sam gave up soccer. Soccer seemed to loosen him up. Although he never talked directly about Dad, he got close to talking about him when they played together like this. She remembered in the early days, just after it happened, when he used to say, "You all right?" or "We'll get there somehow." He didn't explain where "there" was. It was obvious. "There" was the place where life would start to feel normal again. When they wouldn't have lumps in their throats all day.

"Oh, I just needed Max to help me with something," replied Linnea, casually. "I don't think Mom would have approved."

Sam nodded vigorously.

"Yeah, she's weird about him. Like he's going to break or something."

"Sam, do you think she… I mean do you think he…?"

"Yeah. I think so," replied Sam thoughtfully as he lined up his next shot.

Later that evening Sam and Linnea persuaded Mom and Max to play cards. The rickety white kitchen table was dragged out into the courtyard and laid alongside Sam's green bench. Max grabbed two sagging deck chairs and the game began. Sustained by a large bag of sour cream and onion chips, and gallons of soda, Sam proceeded to win every game. Linnea let her mind wander. It was nice to sit in the cool of the evening and watch the tea-light flickering in its jar. Besides the occasional car rumbling down the road, there was nothing to disturb the peace. Birds called to one another in the dusk and the corn in the field opposite swayed gently, turning, as the light faded, to an indistinct gray-green.

Finally, at eleven o'clock, Max announced that he had no intention of losing to Sam any longer and he went to his car to get a cot and sleeping bag. His bed was quickly assembled in the kitchen and everyone turned in for the night. Linnea crawled into her lumpy bed and was soon fast asleep.

As she slept, Linnea dreamed that she was riding Moonlight around and around the yellow farmhouse. The pony was completely serene in her hands and they moved with effortless grace through the night. Suddenly, a girl in red pajamas lay crumpled on the ground in the middle of the field. Linnea knew she had to stop Moonlight and help the girl but the lure of the pony and the night were stronger. Then the girl started moaning and Moonlight turned wild, bucking and rearing as if trying to throw off some memory. Linnea clung terrified to the saddle. Suddenly a barrel organ began to play and Moonlight stiffened and turned into a wooden horse on a merry-go-round. Dad was there, watching and smiling, but for some reason he was waving two sticks of cotton candy like an air traffic controller.

"Stop the ride," he shouted, "she's going to fall!" Linnea looked down and saw an enormous ravine. She began to fall and it was the fall that woke her. Her T-shirt was clammy with sweat, so she rolled out of bed and opened the window. Then she heard a muffled wail coming from the bushes behind the house. Someone was out there, moving around behind the locked wing! She reached for her robe and hurried downstairs.

11: Break-in!

Once she reached the courtyard Linnea stood still and listened. There was definitely someone out there. She stepped back into the kitchen and pushed the door just enough so that it would look closed. Then she peered out from the slightly ajar edge. Max stirred on his cot but didn't wake. Linnea felt reassured just knowing he was there. Now she heard footsteps coming closer. There was a crack over her head as something hit the upstairs window. Crack! There it was again. Then a spray of grit hit the wall and out of the shadows stepped Emmy.

"What are you doing?" hissed Linnea as she slipped out of the front door and held it half-closed behind her.

"Trying to wake you up," grinned Emmy in the half-light.

"Yeah, well, you've done that," said Linnea. "What do you have there?"

"Grandpa's tool box," she replied. "I nearly died trying to get it around the back of your house. You can carry it now. We'll see what sort of noise *you* make when it bangs your shins."

"Thanks," said Linnea dryly. "Why do I need this?"

"I'm taking you off for a little night burglary," Emmy answered.

"Absolutely not," said Linnea setting the toolbox down with a thud. "Not on your life."

"What's the matter, are you scared?" challenged Emmy from behind two long strands of copper hair. She looked like a mischievous moon sprite.

"I'm not breaking into that farmhouse," said Linnea firmly. "It's against the law and Mom would kill me."

"Good," said Emmy, picking up the toolbox and dumping it back into her friend's hands, "because we're not going there. We're going to the playhouse. Still scared?"

Yes, thought Linnea, but she didn't reply. She followed Emmy toward the road and felt the night breeze rustle her pajamas. They were her yellow ones. Dad had brought them back from a trip to Paris. They were too small for her now, but she couldn't bear to throw them out. They were made of brushed cotton. Soft, brushed cotton for Daddy's little girl. She thought again about her dream. Why had she dreamed about a girl in red pajamas?

Once they had walked a hundred yards up the road Linnea had to admit that it was a good night for a break-in. It was warm and the three-quarters moon gave plenty of light. She tilted her head back and looked at the stars. You could see tons here. It wasn't like the constant yellowish glow of the city. Here every point of light was distinct and each star twinkled in its own corner of blackness.

When they reached the riding school, most of the

73

ponies were lying down. Only Ash wandered over to watch them. Linnea's eyes were immediately drawn to the forbidden field where Moonlight lay half veiled by the weeping birch. Linnea was desperate to go and see her, to stroke her soft face and reassure her. It felt like forever since they had been together. Tempting though this was, Linnea decided it would be wiser to stick to the task at hand. Too much lingering would increase their chances of getting caught.

"Not much security, is there?" said Emmy.

"Not much to steal," replied Linnea looking at the battered farm building nervously.

"Emmy, what if the person I saw in the farmhouse comes out and catches us?"

Emmy stopped in her tracks and looked carefully at the building. No lights were on and the curtains were neither open nor shut. She looked at her watch.

"It's one-thirty," she said. "Whoever is in there must be asleep. As long as we're quiet, they'll never know we're here. Anyway, if we do get caught we'll just say that we're taking a shortcut to the coast."

"What if they think we're trying to steal a horse?" asked Linnea.

"Well, if you tried to steal Holly you'd still be trying when the police arrived," said Emmy. They both laughed. Linnea resolved to think of herself as a sleuth and not a thief, but she was glad once they got past the farmhouse.

When they reached the playhouse, Linnea gratefully lowered the toolbox onto the grass.

"So where do we start?" asked Emmy.

"Around the right-hand side," replied Linnea. "There're a couple of peepholes and the planks look looser there. Did you bring a flashlight?"

"Of course," said Emmy, "I'm not stupid."

Each girl took a screwdriver and walked down the side of the shed.

Linnea felt a surge of hot pain on her left ankle.

"Ouch!" she said, "There're stinging nettles." She rubbed her left foot against the sore calf and the friction relieved the pain a little.

"Count six planks from the bottom," said Linnea, "and work it off the frame." She jammed her screwdriver into the corner of the shed and started levering it backwards and forwards. To her surprise the plank came off easily.

"Got it," she called to Emmy. "How's yours?"

"Yup!" said Emmy and they dropped the plank to the ground.

"How many do you think we need to take off?" asked Emmy.

"As few as possible," replied Linnea, "then there'll be less to fix later."

"Let's try the three above this one, then," suggested Emmy.

But something moved in the undergrowth. Both girls froze. Had someone followed them? They heard a rustling sound and Linnea's heart thumped against her ribcage. She looked down the side of the shed toward the farmhouse. It glowed pallid in the moonlight, like a corpse. Then a rabbit hopped around the front of the shed and Linnea breathed a sigh of relief.

Once the last plank had been lowered to the ground Emmy shone her flashlight into the gap.

"Come on," she said, "let's climb in."

Emmy slid in first, followed by Linnea.

"Arghh," protested Linnea, "I think I've got a splinter in my stomach."

As she straightened up, Emmy ran her flashlight around the inside of the shed. The long walls were covered with rosettes. Pink, purple, royal blue, yellow, green, and silver, each one with gilt letters proclaiming success; Hemmerby, Melmo, Christianstad, Falkenburg, Linden, Young Riders Schools Contests, Dressage Meets, Point-to-Points, Trail rides and even horse and dog shows. No competition large or small, local or far away had escaped the attention of the inhabitant of this lair. Each achievement had been savored, remembered and recorded. Linnea walked over to Emmy. She was shining the flashlight on a particularly fragile rosette in faded blue silk.

"Wow," said Emmy. "Some of these are really old. Look! This one was eight years before we were born."

"That one looks a little newer," said Linnea, pointing to a pink one at the end of the row. "Shine the flashlight over there. See, it's a Special Merit from the Melmo Juniors."

"She must have been good to win there," said Emmy enviously. She squatted down and picked up the book that lay with its pages splayed open.

"Yuck," she said. "It's pretty dusty."

Pointers For Point-to-Point, read the title, with

Everything You Need To Succeed. Inside were diagrams of ponies taking improbably high jumps.

Linnea picked up the red shoes. The linings had yellowed but you could still see the impression left by the girl's feet. Apart from the dirty strip of rug and the book there was nothing else in the shed. The unknown girl had kicked off her party shoes and stepped into oblivion.

"So who was she?" whispered Linnea. None of the rosettes bore the name of either the rider or her horse. When they got to the last one, Emmy thumped the wall of the shed in frustration.

"We're getting nowhere," she said, "absolutely nowhere."

"Yes and no," said Linnea quietly. "You haven't been looking at the dates."

"What about them?" asked Emmy, her eyes narrowing with curiosity.

"They start before we were born, but they stop exactly ten years ago."

"Tragedy at Farhult," said Emmy, and she gave a low whistle. "Do you think it was *her*?"

"I don't know," said Linnea, "but it might be." She thought back to the crumpled figure in the red pajamas. Of course it had only been a dream, but could dreams reveal things that had actually happened? She felt a sudden jab of fear.

"Let's get out of here," she said. "This place is giving me the creeps."

12: Who Is That Woman?

The next morning Max went back to the city and Linnea set off for the riding school as usual. When she got there Ruth was fussing over girth straps. They had to be exactly right today because Ruth was planning some cross-country riding. Normally Linnea would have welcomed a change, but today she felt numb. Her hands didn't seem to be talking to her arms and her thighs had lost all grip. Holly noticed the difference at once and was particularly willful.

"For goodness' sake, look where you're going," snapped Ruth as Linnea and Holly veered off the route again and ended up in the undergrowth.

"Lean forwards as you go uphill and backwards as you go downhill," she reminded them as they set off into the birch-tree filled woods.

"I bet you're looking forward to the gymkhana in July," said Elke who had drawn up beside her.

"What gymkhana?" asked Linnea wearily.

"The Melmo Juniors, of course," Elke replied, eyeing Linnea closely. "The biggest contest in the South."

Linnea's mind sped to the pink rosette in the shed.

"Yes, I've heard of it," she said vaguely.

"Ruth won't enter you, so I suppose I shouldn't have mentioned it," continued Elke smoothly.

No, thought Linnea, *you shouldn't have. Now please go away. I can't cope with you today.* She patted Holly's neck and realized as she straightened up that her head was spinning.

"I'll be entering the advanced categories," said Elke casually. "With Jasper, of course."

"Of course," replied Linnea weakly. Jasper, with his long legs and perfect balance was the pick of the ponies at Farhult. Elke and Jasper; the survival of the fittest.

"Still, I guess you could come along and help with tacking up," said Elke. "It's always good to have stable hands."

"Thank you," said Linnea, puzzled by her own words. Why was she thanking Elke?

Elke also looked surprised. She gave Jasper a smart little kick and cantered to the front of the pack.

Oh, great, thought Linnea. *A gymkhana to end all gymkhanas, and I get to tack up.* She imagined the rows of horse trailers and the bustle of riders, the snack stalls and the wailing of little brothers and sisters, the table of rosettes and trophies, and the microphone calling competitors to their events. And she imagined her father standing in the crowd waiting for his girl to compete.

"I'm glad you got the white one, darling. You look like a princess."

"They're called grays, Dad," she explained patiently, "but this one has no name. It's a ghost horse. I'm forbidden to ride her. And I should be wearing red pajamas …"

Linnea heard a rushing sound in her ears. Then there was nothing. Nothing at all.

When she came to she was lying on the bench by the tack shed. Her head was on Emmy's lap and Emmy was peering anxiously at her.

"You just keeled over," she said, "flopped off Holly and onto the ground. We think you fainted."

Linnea lifted her head slightly and saw Ruth holding a cell phone.

"We've called your Mom. She's on her way."

Linnea nodded but didn't speak. Her head was throbbing and she felt hot all over. Bed was all she wanted, and she didn't care if she never saw another pony in her life.

✳ ✳ ✳

The next few days passed slowly. Linnea became intimately acquainted with her lumpy cot and peeling wallpaper. She dozed, daydreamed and spent hours watching a dandelion seed fluttering in a spider's web on the window ledge. She could hear Sam and Mom's voices indistinctly as they worked together in the living room stripping paint off the walls. Trays of lunch or supper were collected from her bedside untouched. She couldn't even face ice cream. On the third day, however, she was better enough to feel restless. At home she would have lain on the sofa and watched TV but there was no TV here. Sam brought her a few of Mom's magazines to read, but Linnea found them dull. How could anyone find so many ads for anti-wrinkle cream interesting?

On the afternoon of the fifth day, Linnea heard Emmy's voice downstairs followed by the unmistakable sound of cowboy boots clomping up the wooden staircase. She sat up and wriggled her twisted sleeping bag until it was smooth.

"Hello, stranger," said Emmy, as she flopped down onto the end of Linnea's bed. She was wearing her favorite leather tasseled pants and Montana T-shirt. Her red hair was in a messy ponytail, probably left over from the day before, but her skin was flushed, making her smile even more dazzling than usual. Linnea was struck by how pretty she was.

"I've brought you something," she said, lifting a large, battered satchel onto the bed.

"Ta-da!" she cried and handed over a wad of paper.

Linnea laid each piece out on her lap. They were charcoal drawings of the gray pony, exquisitely done.

"Wow!" she exclaimed. "Did you do these?"

"Yup," said Emmy.

"I can't believe it," said Linnea. "That's exactly how she looks."

There were sketches of Moonlight grazing by the birch trees, others of her lying down, and one of her standing close to the fence, staring out toward the sea. In each drawing Emmy had captured the pony's sadness.

"How come you're so good at drawing?" asked Linnea.

"Oh, everyone in my family can draw," said Emmy airily. Linnea remembered that Emmy's grandfather was an artist, but the girl had never spoken about anyone else.

"Do you have brothers or sisters?" Linnea asked cautiously.

"No," Emmy replied, and silence fell between the two friends. Linnea listened to the sparrows chirping outside. Suddenly she felt very weak and tired, very small and alone. Here she was in the middle of nowhere, with a girl she hardly knew, chasing after Moonlight's past for reasons that she couldn't fathom. What was the point of it all?

She looked at Emmy and took a deep breath. It was time to explain.

"My father died eighteen months ago," she said. "He was on his motorcycle. He lost control on a sharp bend and rode into a wall. Mom said he wouldn't have felt much." Then she had to stop. Her throat was tight and tears began to flow down her face. At first Emmy did not react at all. She kept on looking straight in front of her.

"Did he love you?" she asked, suddenly turning to face her friend.

Linnea nodded and her now her whole body began to shake with sobs.

"Did you love him?" Emmy continued steadily.

Linnea nodded again. Her heart ached.

"Then that is all that matters," Emmy replied quietly. Linnea nodded. She was too choked up to speak.

"My parents have gone to Montana," Emmy said, tactfully changing the subject. She pulled off the cowboy boots and wriggled her feet under Linnea's sleeping bag. "Dad suddenly got it into his head that he would buy a cattle farm even though he knows nothing about farming." She shook her head ruefully. "My parents have never been practical. Big dreamers." She rolled her eyes.

"Like you, then," smiled Linnea.

"Yeah," admitted Emmy. "My Mom loved the idea. She's quite a famous painter. Grandfather says her work is amazing. He said she should definitely go for the light. Painters are obsessed with light, you know."

Linnea nodded, even though she knew nothing about painters. It was good to hear Emmy talk about her family and she wanted to know more.

"So they both went and grandfather agreed to look after me until they got everything sorted out. Trouble is, that was six months ago."

"So when are you going?" Linnea asked apprehensively.

"I don't know," sighed Emmy. "I get lots of e-mails, but they always say the same thing. More problems on the ranch, more reasons why I have to wait."

"So you're stuck with me for now," said Linnea, poking her friend in the ribs.

"Yes," smiled Emmy. "Thank goodness for that. You can't imagine how awful it was when it was just Elke's gang and the boys." Linnea threw her arms around Emmy.

"I'm really glad I've got you too. Please don't go to Montana just yet, okay?"

Emmy laughed.

"Yeah okay, but you'd better get well. If I have to have another riding lesson without you I'll go crazy!"

13: Max Confesses

The following morning Mom declared that Linnea was better. This meant that she was allowed downstairs where the walls were smooth and damp with fresh plaster. They smelled like wet clay in a school pottery room.

"Look!" said Sam proudly. "We finished!"

"I feel like an earthworm," said Mom.

"Yeah, you look like one," agreed Sam and Mom started laughing. She had dried plaster all over her hair and face. Linnea guessed that she had been up all night plastering.

"I wanted to get it finished," said Mom eagerly. "We must do our best. Max has been so…"

"Hunky?" suggested Sam

"Gorgeous?" suggested Linnea.

"Kind," said Mom blushing deeply. "Honestly I don't know what's gotten into you two," she said, and then she giggled like a happy schoolgirl.

They set up breakfast in the courtyard and basked in the early morning sun. Linnea thought how strange it was that they had settled so quickly into a different routine. Normally the three of them would be out in the city by now, making their way to school and work. But here it felt so normal to be sitting together on Sam's green bench idly watching the wasps trying to get at the jam. Mom had adopted a chipped porcelain bowl as her coffee cup and Sam drank orange juice out of the carton. Linnea gnawed on an extremely stale roll because Sam had forgotten to buy fresh ones. She gazed at her plate. It was pale blue and old-fashioned, but somehow perfect for this place. She looked over to the rustling branches of the apple trees and vowed to live in the countryside when she grew up.

Suddenly they heard a car approaching and a red Alpha Romeo turned into the drive. The passenger door opened and Max scrambled out. Mom's jaw dropped.

"Hello, workers!" he said. Then out of the driver's seat stepped a very tall blonde woman in a white pantsuit.

"This is Anna," said Max cheerfully. "She insisted on meeting you all and seeing how the work is progressing."

Anna stepped forward to shake Mom's hand, but Mom looked self-conscious. She was still in "earthworm" mode. Her ratty old sneakers, vest, T-shirt and purple shorts were covered in plaster.

"I see you've been hard at work," said Anna politely.

Sensing Mom's unease, Max turned to Sam.

"Come on, young man," he said cheerfully, "give us a tour!"

"I'll go to the shop," stammered Mom. "I'm out of coffee." Then she grabbed Linnea's hand, "You come with me," she ordered.

As soon as they were out of earshot Mom started to

shake her head and tut. Linnea knew from experience that this was a bad sign.

"For goodness sake! Look at the state of me! Why didn't he call? Who on *earth* is that woman? Who on earth is that *woman*?"

Linnea decided that the blonde in the pantsuit was definitely the worst part of the situation, and that it would be better to focus Mom's attention on coffee and sprucing herself up.

"Mom," she said, "you walk down to the village and I'll sneak back to the house and get your swimming things. Then you can have a quick dip in the sea while I buy the coffee."

"Coffee?" said Mom incredulously. "Do you really think I ran out of coffee? Have I ever run out of coffee in your entire life?"

Linnea was forced to admit that such an emergency had never arisen.

"Of course I haven't run out of coffee," hissed Mom "I just had to get away from that *woman* so I could think."

"Look, Mom," said Linnea in her most matter-of-fact tone, "we don't know that Anna's actually his girlfriend. She could be a friend or something."

Mom closed her eyes and took three deep, calming breaths. Then she said, "Okay. Linnea, we'll go with your plan. Get my swimming stuff. It's hanging on the line behind the shed. Get my red T-shirt dress while you're there. Now go. *Go*."

Linnea dashed up the drive as fast as she could. As

she ran she wondered about Mom's makeup. Where was it? Would it be too obvious that Mom liked Max if she came back from the village store looking ravishing? She reached the cottage just in time to see Sam leading Max and Anna down his path to the sea.

"Rats!" cursed Linnea. She burst into the house and grabbed Mom's makeup bag from the windowsill. Then she seized the red dress and tore the swimming stuff off the line.

Mom had almost reached the village by the time Linnea caught up with her. She was walking very fast and looked agitated.

"You'll have to go further around the headland," panted Linnea. "Sam's taken them down his path to the beach." Mom groaned, grabbed her things, and set off at a run.

"Can't do the makeup," she called over her shoulder. "Haven't got a mirror!"

Linnea got back to the cottage to find Sam showing off the new plaster.

"It took us *hours*," he declared, "probably about four whole days."

"Ah, Linnea," said Max, "I see you got fresh cakes in honor of our guest."

"Yes" said Linnea, trying to sound hospitable when all she really wanted to do was wring Max's neck.

The coffee was brewed and the cakes were laid out but still Mom didn't come. The three of them sat at the courtyard table. Linnea knew she ought to make polite conversation, but she couldn't think what to say. Anna asked Sam a few questions about school and he answered grudgingly. During a particularly awkward pause an orchestra struck up inside Anna's handbag.

"Sorry," she said, "I'll have to take that." She walked toward the road clutching the phone to her ear.

At this point Mom returned.

"Nice dress," said Max.

"Thanks," said Mom, as if it were the most normal thing in the world to go buy coffee in shorts and return in a dress.

"Have you known Anna long?" she asked in a carefully neutral voice.

"Of course," replied Max as he bit into a chocolate muffin. "She's a doctor. I think she's just received a call from the hospital."

"I see," said Mom, "do they call her away for emergencies?"

Linnea prayed for an emergency.

"Constantly," said Max with a sigh. "I worry that she works too hard, so I thought a few days down here would be just the thing."

"Just the thing," agreed Mom in a very strange-sounding voice.

"Oh, don't worry about beds and so on," said Max hastily. "We brought a tent so we'll just camp in the garden."

"Oh fine, fine," said Mom who now looked as if she had swallowed poison ivy.

The rest of the day was the worst that Linnea could remember. Max took Anna off for a long walk to look at some "old haunts." Mom disappeared upstairs to rest and refused to come down again. Sam went off to his beloved soccer ground and Linnea was instructed to bike to the fish market in Hemmerby to get some halibut for dinner. She put Mom's purse in her backpack and set off.

The worst thing about biking to Hemmerby was that there was nothing to take Linnea's mind off the enormous problem of Anna. Everything had seemed so hopeful between Max and Mom, but now it was clear that they had been misled, maybe deliberately. Linnea felt angry. Max had led Mom on, and it just wasn't fair.

"I think it's your turn," said a woman behind her in line. Linnea recognized the voice at once. It was Tilda Johnston.

She went to the counter and ordered her fish. The halibut, who still had his head on, looked at Linnea resentfully with his dead eye. Linnea shivered and rummaged in Mom's purse for the money while a large woman with red fingers wrapped the fish in paper and loaded it into a blue and white striped plastic bag.

"Your dad better?" Tilda asked, as she waited for a lanky, long-haired boy to weigh out some shrimp.

"No," said Linnea. "He's dead." Then she ran out of the store before the bewildered physiotherapist could ask her any more questions.

When Linnea got home, Max was sitting in the orchard reading the paper. He looked up when she arrived and smiled.

"Come and join me after you put the fish away," he said. "I made a pot of tea. Grab a mug." Linnea slung the defenseless fish angrily into the fridge and took the smallest mug she could find.

"I'm coming to realize that this is the most perfect spot in the whole world," declared Max, who was leaning back in his chair and looking up at the puffy white clouds.

It was until you turned up, thought Linnea.

"Where's Mom?" she asked pointedly.

"Got a headache," said Max, "I offered her some tea but she says she doesn't touch the stuff."

"Coffee," said Linnea. "Mom drinks coffee."

Max shook his head disapprovingly. "Coffee's not good for headaches."

Then he looked at Linnea over the brim of his teacup.

"So how are the investigations going?" he asked raising one eyebrow conspiratorially.

"None of your business," said Linnea. She surprised herself with the anger in her voice.

Max set his teacup down sharply, missing the saucer and spilling the contents onto the grass.

"Drat!" he said. "Want me to pour you one?"

Linnea held her cup out to be filled and noted with satisfaction that Max's hands trembled slightly.

"I thought we were friends," he said, looking anxiously at her.

"I thought you liked Mom," said Linnea holding his gaze and taking a sip of tea.

"Oh dear," said Max. "I hoped we wouldn't have to have this conversation."

"Well, do you or don't you?" asked Linnea, stirring her tea vigorously.

"What should I say?" asked Max. He seemed to be asking for help again.

"The truth," said Linnea impatiently. "The truth is always the right answer."

"I think your mother is the most special person I have ever met," replied Max.

"Do you like her?" pressed Linnea.

"I've loved your mother since the day I met her," said Max and the anxiety was still in his eyes.

Linnea felt her whole body slacken with relief. The relief was so enormous it passed through her like a tidal wave. Mom was loved. Really loved by this man. He loved her and maybe his love would make her happy again and smile again and sit on the hoods of cars again. Maybe in time some of this dreadful grief would be replaced by something new. The thought of it was too much for her. She burst into tears and ran into the house.

Coffee time had been awkward but dinner was worse. Max looked like a cat on a hot tin roof. His secret was out but he seemed afraid of what Linnea would do with her new knowledge. Linnea was equally unsure. Although Max's admission had solved one set of problems, it had created a whole set of new ones. When would he tell Anna that it was Mom he loved? Or would he tell Mom first? Or would he tell neither of them and muddle on? Or did he expect Linnea to tell Mom? Mom hardly spoke during the meal. She still complained of a headache, but Linnea knew that she was really suffering from confusion. Sam also got quiet when things got tricky, so Linnea asked Anna about her work. It seemed the only safe topic.

Anna seemed quite unaware of the emotional disarray she had unleashed. She complimented Mom on the fish and admired the jug of wild roses on the table. She chatted happily about her work at a children's hospital. At last the evening drew to a close and Linnea sank into bed, relieved that they had, somehow, survived the day.

14: C.M's Saddle

The next morning Linnea woke at five o'clock. She lay in bed for a few minutes, hoping to go back to sleep, but her mind was too active and her thoughts kept turning to Max and Anna. So, moving as quietly as possible, she got dressed and tiptoed downstairs with her sneakers in her hands.

The air outside was fresh and cool. Linnea took a deep breath and savored the scent of cow parsley that grew in thick banks on either side of the driveway. Rather than going the usual way, past the orchard and onto the road, she decided to walk behind the house and investigate Sam's route to the coast. As she skirted the peeling walls, wet grass lapped against her legs and branches from un-pruned trees caught her hair. No wonder Emmy had struggled to get the toolbox through here.

When Linnea got past the building she found a path running between two fields of long grass. This seemed promising. The ground fell away from her, sloping gently toward the sea. A few gulls flew overhead craw crawing to each another. Now the path led into a birch grove and turned sharply right so that it ran parallel to the coast.

Linnea followed it until she reached a stile. Here the path pointed again toward the sea. Something moved behind the trees to the right and made her jump. Then she saw the flank of a large animal. Was it a cow or a bull? The creature moved again and she realized that she must be at the far corner of the riding school. Her heart quickened.

Trampling wild raspberry brambles under foot, she reached the fence and there stood Moonlight. She held out her hand and Moonlight came over at once and nuzzled her shoulder. She slithered into the field, picked a handful of grass, and then held it out on her palm. Linnea felt Moonlight's warm breath on her skin as the pony took the food.

"Wait here," she said with sudden determination, "I'll get some tack." She snaked her way under the fence on the other side and the Farhult ponies began to cluster around her.

"Sorry, I can't stop now," Linnea explained brushing past Gulla and Redlegs. She guessed that Ruth kept her keys in the trailer and decided to start the search there. She ran up the rusting steps two at a time and unlatched the battered doors. The trailer was dark inside and the little anteroom was stacked with faded gossip magazines and crates of empty soda bottles. Ruth tolerated these and claimed that they would soon be taken away for recycling. Linnea doubted it. An environment of neglect got into your brain after a while and you began to think it was normal to climb over piles of garbage to find a riding hat that didn't even fit. Linnea found the shelf where Ruth kept her log. The dog-eared exercise book she used had been stuffed into an old ice cream tub. There was also a sunhat, a tube of sunscreen and a small padlock key. "Got it!" she said triumphantly. Then, humming to herself, she unlocked the shed and slipped the key into her pocket.

She decided that Jasper's equipment would probably be worth trying first. Elke had chosen the best pony, Jasper, so it seemed likely that she had also nabbed the best tack. Sure enough the saddle looked sturdy and all the straps were intact. Linnea heaved it off the floor and staggered outside. As she laid it on the grass she noticed that one corner was embossed with initials. She ran her finger over the letters. "C.M." she said out loud. Then she turned over each flap and buckle hoping to find more but there was nothing. She was sure she had never seen initials on any other riding school equipment. She turned the saddle upside down and found the manufacturer's label: "Liddington Saddles. Est.1784." Linnea gasped. She had heard of these saddles, but never touched one. They were the most expensive saddles that money could buy. She picked it up, more respectfully this time, and waddled to the forbidden field. Moonlight was waiting for her.

"Pleased to see me?" she panted. "Look! I've brought you a fancy saddle!" She lowered it to the ground and felt the sweat rolling down her forehead. Getting the saddle through the fence would be like getting a fly through a spider's web. The alternative was to toss it over the top. But "tossing" would only work for something light. This saddle was heavy, and Linnea winced at the thought of the barbed wire tearing into the leather. For a few minutes she and the pony looked helplessly at each another.

"Moonlight, Moonlight," she crooned, holding her hand over the top of the fence, "tell me what to do about this enormous saddle." The pony again pushed her nose into Linnea's hand and nuzzled her.

Then Linnea noticed an old oil drum in the main field. She ran over to it and tipped it onto one edge so that it could be rolled along. She had seen Ruth do this setting up jumps for point-to-point. The drum moved easily and Linnea maneuvered it as far as Moonlight's fence. Next she stood the saddle on its end and climbed onto the drum, which wobbled slightly but took her weight. Now it was time for the tricky part. She levered the saddle off the ground and pressed it to her chest, then she twisted her upper body so that the saddle hung over the top of the fence. Squeezing her eyes shut, she dropped it. To her relief it fell straight down into Moonlight's field without touching the wire twists. Then she lay on her belly and began to lizard back into the field.

Later, looking back on that morning, Linnea wondered when she had passed the point of no return. It was hard to say. But certainly the saddle hadn't helped. It fit Moonlight like a glove. The sun had risen higher in the sky and Linnea felt its heat on her back. The grass was dry underfoot and the occasional rumbling of cars on the main road began to interrupt the silence. Linnea checked her watch. It was seven-thirty. Ruth might come early. Was there still time? Then she looked back at Moonlight, saddled and ready to go. The temptation was too great.

Putting her left foot into the stirrup, she mounted and took the reins. Moonlight whinnied and her whole body seemed to tighten with anticipation.

"Just a little walk," Linnea said, "nothing fancy, okay?" Then she smiled as the pony set off. Asking this pony not to be fancy was like asking a ballerina not to dance. The walk led into a trot, which flowed into a canter and finally burst into a gallop. Every inch of Moonlight came alive with the forgotten joy of speed. Around and around they flew, Moonlight's hooves pounding the dry earth beneath them. It was exhilarating, liberating, perfect. Linnea wanted to ride like this forever, but the more she tried to hold onto the moment the more fragile it seemed. Old worries and thoughts seeped back into her mind and the spell was broken. Moonlight's pace slowed to a canter, to a trot, to a walk and then she stopped. Linnea had questioned the magic and now it was gone. She dismounted and pressed her face into Moonlight's neck.

"I'm sorry," she whispered. Moonlight was breathing hard and foamy saliva bubbled next to her bit, but she quivered with life.

"I'll come back," said Linnea. "And I'll get you out of here, I promise."

She unsaddled the pony and struggled back across the field, feeling drained. She lugged the equipment back into the gloomy shed and breathed in the smell of mud, leather and riding boots. Then she returned Ruth's key to its ice cream tub in the trailer, laid her riding hat on the bench and slumped onto the floor. "Marriage of Prince

Berthild to Childhood Sweetheart, Exclusive Photos,"
proclaimed one of the magazines, "Bikini Styles For Fuller
Figures," suggested another. Linnea began flicking through
"Beauty Chat." Maybe she would stay here till the others
arrived? But as she tried to read an article on pedicures she
realized that she couldn't stay. Even the thought of riding
Holly was ridiculous after this morning. She dropped the
magazine and walked out into the daylight.

As her eyes adjusted to the brightness, someone stepped
out from behind the trailer door and threw a sack over her
head. She tried to scream, but fear stifled all sound. "Down
the steps," ordered a wheezy woman's voice.

15: Eva

A hand on the small of Linnea's back prodded her forwards. The fibers of the sack were scratchy and dust tickled the back of her throat. After twenty paces she heard the woman open a door.

"In here," she rasped, "sit down." Gingerly, Linnea bent her knees. There was a scraping sound and then she felt the edge of a chair behind her legs, so she sat. Her heart was beating fast and her palms were sticky. She heard the door shut. Then she felt two hands on her shoulders and the sack was lifted.

Her captor, a thin woman with dark eyes, peered at her.

"So you're Ruth's charity case," she said, gripping the back of Linnea's chair with a gnarled hand, "trespassing."

Her face was sallow and she had deep worry lines etched around her eyes. Around her neck she wore three gold chains covered in charms which made her look like a gypsy, a thin, hungry gypsy.

"Are you…?" Linnea began.

"This is the third time you've come outside of riding hours," continued Mrs. Malmgren. "This is my land and I have a right to my privacy." She was breathing heavily and her face was so close that Linnea could smell the coffee on her breath. "So I shall ban you from the riding school." She tried to lean down closer toward Linnea, but this seemed to constrict her lungs too much and she started to cough noisily. She sank into a chair at the kitchen table, put a hand on her chest and closed her eyes. All her energy was now focused on drawing breath.

Linnea scanned the room. The faded gray-blue curtains were closed, so the sun shone in slithers across the floorboards and dust danced in each shaft of light. There was a very simple kitchen at this end of the room: a large farmhouse sink with a small dish drain, a rickety-looking stove and a few wall-mounted cupboards. Piles of food boxes were wedged between the tops of the cupboards and the bowing ceiling. A lumpy couch and two small easy chairs with wooden arms lay at the far end of the room.

Linnea looked back at Mrs. Malmgren. She wore a coral sweatshirt over brown leggings and her gray-brown hair was pulled back into a messy braid which probably dated from the day before.

"Would you like some water?" Linnea suggested.

Eva Malmgren fluttered one hand dismissively.

"I know. I'll open a window," said Linnea. "I think you need some air." A smell of burnt toast, old coffee and unmade beds pervaded the farmhouse and Linnea wondered if Mrs. Malmgren ever aired the place.

"No," she protested.

Reluctantly Linnea sat down again.

"You should see a doctor about your cough," she said.

Eva swiveled around in her chair and looked at Linnea sullenly. Her breathing had settled into a quieter rhythm now.

"What's your game?" she said moodily. "Why don't you just clear off to the beach like everyone else? It's the summer vacation, isn't it? What's the matter with you?"

Linnea was riled now.

"I could ask you the same question," she said half rising from her seat. "What are you doing in this gloomy old farmhouse? What's the big drama? Why is Mrs. Malmgren trying to hide away for the rest of her life?"

Eva stood up again and walked toward Linnea, wagging a bony finger at her.

"Nobody talks to me like that," she growled.

"That's probably because nobody talks to you at all," protested Linnea. "You never go out. And you should. The riding school is falling to pieces and the ponies are neglected. Everything needs a good cleaning and a coat of paint. And as for the way you've treated the beautiful white pony in the far field, don't get me started!"

Mrs. Malmgren's jaw dropped in amazement.

"How dare you?" she cried. "How dare you?" But this time her anger was too much for her. Her breathing began to tighten again and she staggered over to the couch and lay down, gasping like a fish out of water.

Linnea ran over and slipped a cushion under Eva's head. Close up she could see some of the charms around Eva's neck; there were horseshoes, tiny pony figurines, golden roses, an angel, a tree and various leaf-shapes.

"Don't get upset," she said gently. "Just rest." Eva nodded

slightly. She had closed her eyes and was concentrating on drawing each breath.

Linnea glanced at the knitting on the coffee table. There was a pale blue scarf three quarters finished and a lime green mitten. Then she looked at the newspapers and saw, to her surprise, that they were recent. Lifting up a plate of dried up sandwiches, she found a novel with a bookmark sticking out of it. The cover showed a heroine in a flowing white dress being kissed by a cavalry officer. Then she noticed a cushion lying on the floor next to the coffee table. It depicted a gray pony standing in a kaleidoscope swirl of color, carefully sewn in cross-stitch.

"Did you make this?" she asked, picking it up and bringing it to Mrs. Malmgren's side.

Eva opened one eye and then nodded imperceptibly.

"Is it the gray pony in the field outside?" she pressed.

Eva nodded again. Linnea took her hand and squeezed it.

"I should have had the pony destroyed," Eva said. "The vet in Hemmerby is an old flame of mine. He would have come. But I never… I couldn't."

"Tell me what happened," prompted Linnea. "What did the pony do?"

But Eva turned her head away.

"Go!" she said.

"But Mrs. Malmgren," Linnea protested, "Your chest…"

Mrs. Malmgren gave Linnea a searching look.

"You're a kind little thing, aren't you?" she said. "But I do need to be alone. Please go now."

"Mrs. Malmgren," replied Linnea "you did nothing wrong. I'm sure of that."

Eva smiled bitterly.

"Clear off, kid," she said. "Forget the ban, but no more snooping, okay?"

Linnea nodded.

"Thank you for letting me ride here," she said simply. She put her chair back at the kitchen table and let herself out.

It was eight o'clock, and the other riders would arrive soon. Linnea decided that she needed time to think so she walked through the pony field and back onto the main road. There was no point going home; the atmosphere would still be strained. If Sam had any sense he would stay out of the way. Maybe Max could spend some time with Anna and explain the situation? Or maybe Mom and Anna could settle the matter between themselves? Linnea tried to think what happened at school when two girls thought they had the same boyfriend. It was usually messy and the boy would end up saying he didn't like either of them. Linnea shuddered. She headed down the road toward the village. It would be good to talk things over with Emmy. She might have ideas about how to handle the Max situation and she would certainly want to hear about meeting Mrs. Malmgren.

16: Eyes

Linnea approached an old man sitting on the veranda. He drank coffee from a yellow enamel mug and gazed out to sea. His features were craggy and weather-beaten and his long white hair and bushy beard made him look like a picture of Abraham that Linnea had seen once in Sunday School. He wore faded denim jeans splattered with paint.

"Excuse me," she began, "I've come to see Emmy."

The old man did not react so Linnea tried again, a little louder this time, in case the man was deaf.

"Sorry to disturb you. I've come to see Emmy."

"Never heard of her," said the old man, looking out to sea.

"But this is her address," protested Linnea.

"No Emmy living here," replied the man, looking at her for the first time. He had one green eye and one blue. Linnea had never seen anyone with different colored eyes before and she wondered if it was natural.

"Siv lives here," he said suddenly. "Do you want to see her?"

Linnea remembered Emmy's real name and blushed.

"Yes," she said eagerly. "Yes, I've come to see Siv."

The old man pushed through the doors behind him and disappeared into the house, but Linnea wasn't sure if she was supposed to follow. She stepped onto the veranda and hovered nervously, hoping that Emmy would appear. After a few minutes he returned with a large can.

"Sit down if you like," he said. Then he went back to his seat on the veranda and started looking out to sea again. Linnea perched on the edge of the nearest chair. A few minutes passed but Emmy did not come. Linnea cleared her throat.

"Is she here?" she asked cautiously.

"Depends," replied the man. Linnea was confused.

"Doesn't she *want* to see me?"

"Maybe," answered the man. But now he looked at her more kindly and a smile played at the corners of his mouth.

"So you're Em, I mean Siv's grandfather," Linnea began.

"No," said the old man, "I'm not."

"Oh! Where is her grandfather, then?" asked Linnea.

"Dead or useless," said the old man, "one of the two." Linnea began to feel irritated.

"So who are you?" she asked.

"Siv's grandfather," replied the old man.

Linnea bit her tongue. They were going around in circles. Maybe the old man had lost his marbles.

"Siv has lived with me since the twelfth of January," said the old man with sudden precision. He opened his box which was full of pastels. Many of them were worn down to stubs. He pulled a piece of paper out of his pocket and smoothed it onto his lap.

"Too small, really," he said as he started to make a few strokes with a piece of charcoal.

"Does she have family in Montana?" asked Linnea, determined to get sense out of the old man.

"Elouise-Mathilde," replied the old man.

"Who's that?" asked Linnea.

"A beautiful woman I used to know," he replied. "Looks just like her."

"Who does?" pressed Linnea.

"Who's asking?" said the old man, reaching for a yellow pastel.

Linnea sighed. "Do you know who I am?" she asked. "Does Siv talk about me?"

"All the time, all the time," said the old man, leaning back into his chair and looking out to sea again.

"You have a very high forehead," he said, tossing a pastel back into the box, "and you don't know how to sit for a portrait." Then he handed her the piece of paper.

At first Linnea couldn't make any sense of the picture. Colors swirled all over it in every direction but then a single eye stared out from the mass of tangled threads, and Linnea recognized it as her own.

"Why did you only do my eye?" she asked.

"Because that is how I see you," he replied.

"Are you trying to tell me I'm nosy?"

"I didn't draw your nose, did I?" He laughed. "So what *are* you looking for?"

"Siv" she replied.

"I didn't say who, I said what."

Linnea paused for a minute. "I want Mom to be happy

again and I want her to marry Max so that Sam will have someone to play soccer with. And I want to know what Moonlight did wrong and why she is being punished. Then maybe I can do something about it." She doubted the old man would understand, but she was getting tired of his strange ways.

"That's quite a bit," he said, "quite a bit." Then he walked into the house, closed the door and locked it. There was no choice. It was time to go home and find out if Mom and Max had straightened things out.

17: An Emergency At Farhult

When Linnea got home she found Anna in the courtyard, sunbathing. She was sitting in a deck chair sipping apple juice. Although she was quite tanned the tops of her arms were pale and her stomach was white.

"Where is everyone?" Linnea asked.

"Gone to the stores in Hemmerby."

"Why didn't you go with them?"

"Because I think they've gone to buy my birthday cake," laughed Anna.

"Oh," said Linnea. "I didn't know it was your birthday. Weren't you hoping for something a little more…romantic?"

"Well I'm single right now," said Anna sitting up and looking at Linnea quizzically, "so …"

"Single?" said Linnea. Her voice sounded shrill with surprise. "But I thought…"

"That Max was my boyfriend?"

"Yeah."

"We've been through this with your Mom," said Anna. "Max sent you a postcard from the city, saying that we were coming and explaining about me, but apparently you haven't been looking in your mailbox."

"Never thought to check it," Linnea said. "Where is it, anyway?"

Anna laughed.

"It's on the road, but admittedly the bushes have grown over it a bit."

"So you're not…" began Linnea.

"No," said Anna firmly. "I'm his cousin."

Linnea could have jumped for joy. She wanted to throw her arms around Anna and say, "Thank you, thank you, thank you."

"Max was very eager for me to meet your mom," Anna continued. She pushed her sunglasses onto the top of her head and squinted at Linnea.

"Oh," said Linnea.

Then Anna started rubbing sunscreen on her long, smooth legs. Suddenly Linnea's mind jumped to Eva Malmgren in her strange-looking brown leggings and she felt a rush of fear.

"I know you're a children's doctor," she said, "but can you do grownups too?"

Anna smiled. "Why do you ask?"

"If someone's breath sounded wheezy and they sometimes struggled to breathe, what would be wrong with them?" she asked. Anna put the sunscreen down sharply.

"Is this a real case?" she asked. Linnea nodded.

"I would assume heart or lung trouble and call a doctor immediately."

Linnea felt herself go hot with panic.

"Come now," she ordered. Anna got to her feet at once and followed Linnea as she ran onto the road.

"What's this about?" she asked.

"You'll see when we get there," panted Linnea.

The two of them pounded down the road toward the riding school. The sun was high in the sky and Linnea was sweating with heat and fear. She burst through the gate and into the first field. To her relief Anna kept up with her easily but her heart sank when she saw Ruth standing by the trailers with two adult riders.

"What are you doing here?" she shouted. Linnea pretended not to hear and ran toward the back door of the house.

"That's private property," yelled Ruth, "you're not allowed in there." Linnea wrenched the door handle, but it was locked. Ruth was now running toward them, looking furious. In desperation Linnea pressed her nose against the dirty window and saw the one thing she dreaded to see. Eva was slumped on the floor by the back door.

"She's collapsed!" Linnea shrieked. Anna peered in as well.

"Is the door locked?" she asked. Linnea nodded. Anna stooped down and picked up a log.

"Stand back," she said.

"Put that down," ordered Ruth. "I don't know what you're doing but that woman is not to be disturbed under *any* circumstances."

I'm a doctor," said Anna firmly, "and I'm telling you to stand back." With that she lifted the log as high as she could and threw it through the window. The glass shattered and fell into the house although much of it was left in jagged shards clinging to the edges of the window frame. Anna put her hand in carefully and felt for the latch. At last the window was fully open.

"Linnea, give me a boost," Anna instructed, but Ruth got down on her knees first.

"I'm sorry," she said, "I didn't realize. I'll do this. I'm stronger than Linnea." Anna put her right foot into Ruth's cupped hands and got her left foot onto the window ledge. In one bound she was in. Linnea and Ruth watched from the window as she bent over and felt Eva's neck.

"She's still alive," said Anna, "but her pulse is very faint. We need an ambulance." They all reached into their pockets but Anna found her cell phone first. Ruth knelt down again.

"Climb in, Linnea" she said. "We need to find the back door key." Linnea nodded. With Ruth's help she got both feet onto the window ledge. Then she jumped down, narrowly missing a large sheet of broken glass as she landed. She approached Eva cautiously.

"Mrs. Malmgren," she said gently, "Mrs. Malmgren?" She touched her slim shoulder, but Eva Malmgren did not stir. Linnea gazed for a moment at the woman she knew so little about. Suddenly she noticed something sticking out from under Eva's arm. It was the key.

"Here," she said and tossed it to Ruth who by now had climbed in too. Ruth tugged the back door open and they stood in the doorway together looking toward the road.

"Will the ambulance get here soon?" asked Linnea anxiously.

"Any minute" replied Ruth. "I'd better tell my students to go home."

Linnea turned back into the house. Some plates were drying on the drain next to the sink but there was no food out except for a small bowl of grapes on the table. How did Mrs. Malmgren live? She was sure Eva never went to the store. She opened the fridge. There was food inside: a package of ham, a bowl of meatballs, some cheese, a box of chocolate and a half gallon of milk.

"Linnea, we need to notify next of kin," said Anna after she had finished talking on the phone. "Can you help me look for an address book?"

Linnea glanced around the room and decided to begin with the large pine dresser against the far wall. She rifled through a drawer of old perfume bottles, a drawer of wool and a drawer of carpentry tools. Then she tried the cupboards below. The first was full of large photo albums. This made her fingers itch with curiosity. Perhaps there would be photos of the riding school in its glory days, or even photos of the girl who played in the pink playhouse? Perhaps there were photos of C.M., who owned the fancy saddle? Then she felt guilty for wanting to pry so she pushed the albums back into place and tackled the next cupboard. Here she found a pink telephone with its wire wrapped neatly round it. Underneath were some battered brown phonebooks and a thin red notebook.

"Got the address book. Who do we call?" she cried.

"Malmgrens" said Ruth as she filled a glass of water at the sink. "Jonas, Lotta and Carolina. They live in Hemmerby now."

Linnea flicked through the pages looking for "M" and then found Jonas.

"Malmgren, 56 Gullway?" she asked.

"Yes," replied Ruth.

"Do you want me to call?" Anna asked. Linnea's throat felt dry. She shook her head and began to dial. *I'm going to know now*, she thought. *This is it.*

"Carolina Malmgren," said the voice on the other end of the line. Linnea's heart skipped a beat. C.M! It was C.M!

"Are you a relative of Eva Malmgren?" she asked.

"Yes, I'm her granddaughter," the woman replied, but her voice sounded guarded.

"I'm afraid I have bad news," said Linnea. "Eva has collapsed and her pulse is very weak. The doctor is here and an ambulance is on its way."

"It's very serious," hissed Anna.

"You need to get to Hemmerby hospital right now," continued Linnea, trying to keep her voice as calm as possible, "Eva is seriously ill."

"We have no contact with Eva," replied Carolina coolly.

Linnea felt a surge of anger, "Eva may be dying," she protested.

"Thank you for telling us, but I suggest you call someone else," said Carolina firmly, and before Linnea could reply, she hung up.

18: Ruth's Tale

A few minutes later they heard sirens approaching.

"Oh thank goodness," said Anna. Linnea and Ruth followed her out and watched as four paramedics in green pants and fluorescent yellow jackets came running through the pony field with a stretcher. They were big, burly men but they moved quickly and soon they were squeezing through the narrow farmhouse door.

"Who do we have here?" asked the tallest paramedic, a well built man with a closely shaven head and a bristly ginger moustache. He picked up Eva's wrist to take her pulse.

"Okay, steady, guys. We'll have to take her in." Very gently they lifted Eva Malmgren onto the stretcher and one of them put an oxygen mask over her mouth and nose. She looked like a damaged bird, small and impossibly frail. Linnea ran to the stretcher with the cushion of Moonlight in the swirl of color.

"Here," she said, "take this." The oldest of the four men, who had graying hair and kindly eyes, took the cushion and smiled.

"Someone put a lot of fine stitching into that," he said,

admiring the white pony against its blue sky. Then he slipped it onto the stretcher above Eva's head and they set off.

Linnea, Anna and Ruth followed the stretcher out and watched the men carry it back through the field to the waiting ambulance. *Finally, Mrs. Malmgren leaves Farhult*, thought Linnea.

There was an uneasy pause once the ambulance had gone. It seemed disrespectful to go straight back to business-as-usual.

"I think I'll head back to the summer house and see if everyone's home from Hemmerby," said Anna eventually. "I'll tell your Mom where you are, if you want?" Linnea nodded and smiled her thanks.

"What about some tea, Linnea?" suggested Ruth. "It will revive us. I'll put in lots of sugar." Linnea thought it was strange to make tea in someone else's house, especially when that person had just been rushed to the hospital, but Ruth seemed very much at home in this kitchen. She located the teabags, mugs and teaspoons instantly.

"So you're the one who's been looking after Mrs. Malmgren," said Linnea, "buying her food and stuff."

Ruth nodded and tucked her sandy hair behind her ears.

"It goes with the job," she said. So that explained why Tilda had been so eager to protect the old lady from any disturbance. Tilda and Ruth had both seen to it that Eva Malmgren's escape from the world was complete.

"Has nobody thought that Mrs. Malmgren needs

help?" challenged Linnea. "And I don't mean shopping, I mean getting out of this rotten old farmhouse and enjoying the world again."

Ruth sighed. "Linnea, you don't understand."

"Don't I?" countered Linnea.

Ruth poured tea into two chipped mugs and brought them over to the couch.

"You're a determined little cookie, aren't you?"

Linnea rubbed her wrists. They hurt from lugging the saddle to Moonlight's field. She had never thought of herself as determined before. Losing Dad had made her feel wobbly inside, but perhaps feeling so vulnerable *had* made her more determined.

"Milk-bucket was the finest pony money could buy…" Ruth began.

"Milk-bucket!" spluttered Linnea. "They called her *Milk-bucket*?"

"Yes," said Ruth briskly, "now don't interrupt. As I said, Milk-bucket was top-class."

Still is, thought Linnea indignantly, but she kept quiet this time.

"Eva bought her for Carolina's sixteenth birthday, when it was obvious that the girl was really serious about her riding."

"So she was good," prompted Linnea.

"Oh yes," said Ruth, "won everything. She was, I mean is, little. Lightweight like her grandma, with nerves of steel, of course. Nobody could touch her on Milk-bucket. She just cleaned up at the shows. Won every medal."

116

Linnea nodded. This much she knew from the walls of the playhouse.

"So there was never any reason to think…" Ruth's voice faltered slightly, but she gathered herself. "There was never any reason to think that the pony couldn't be trusted."

Linnea held her breath.

"But it all went wrong at the Melmo Juniors." Ruth looked out of the window toward the birch trees as if summoning the memory from somewhere deep within the woods.

"That year it was held at Farhult and everyone was so excited. The Melmo Juniors rotates around each club so you only get to host it once every ten years. We were sure that Carolina would win the cup. The local paper sent a reporter and even the village school took the afternoon off. We were all expecting her to triumph. That's what made it so cruel."

"What was so cruel?" breathed Linnea.

"She was thrown. Thrown at the final jump of the last heat. Milk-bucket suddenly lost it. He started bucking and rearing as if he had seen a ghost. Carolina fell and she um… she…" Ruth's voice was getting hoarse. "She landed badly. Broke her neck." There was a pause.

"Is she…"

"Paralyzed," said Ruth. "The family never forgave the pony and they never forgave Eva, either."

"But," protested Linnea, "surely if it had been reliable up until that day then…"

"I know, I know," sighed Ruth, "but people don't

117

always think logically in these situations. The farm was sold and the family moved to a ground floor apartment in Hemmerby, close to medical help for Carolina and…"

"Eva has been a recluse ever since."

"Yes, I think it's her way of punishing herself."

Linnea buried her face in her hands. Why did things have to be like this? So much unnecessary suffering.

Ruth got up.

"So now you know," she said. "I've got my next class now. I think you'd better go home, don't you?"

"Just one thing," said Linnea as she stood up. "Was Carolina wearing red pajamas that day?" Ruth's eyes widened with surprise.

"For a point-to-point? No, of course not! Why do you ask?"

"Oh nothing," shrugged Linnea, "it was just some silly dream I had."

"Now listen," said Ruth, "you've done a good job here this morning, there's no denying it. But it's time to leave the past alone. Don't you think?"

Not on your life, thought Linnea. *I'm just getting started*. She had to prove Moonlight's reliability. She was sure of that now, and an idea was beginning to take shape in her mind.

19: Action!

Carolina Malmgren sat by the telephone and stared out of the window. A few teenage boys had gathered at the bus stop across the street. They looked as if they had sneaked out of school early. Carolina's hands lay idle in her lap but her mind was busy. So Grandma was ill. Seriously ill. She thought back to the last time she had seen Eva. That time it had been Carolina who had been in the hospital. Grandma had refused to believe that her granddaughter's legs were as bad as the doctors said. But that day, Dad had been brutally frank.

"You've got to face it. We all have. That pony has seriously hurt Carolina, and she's paralyzed from the waist down. That pony…"

They hadn't seen Grandma again after that. Dad said that it was guilt, that it served her right and that the old woman should have been more careful about the ponies she gave people to ride. And at the time Carolina had been too preoccupied to think any more about it; there had been endless physiotherapy and doctor's appointments, then the move to Hemmerby and learning how to get around in a wheelchair. There had been visits from friends who didn't know what to say, and then the long, long adjustment to a new life in which riding would never again play a part. Carolina sighed and wondered about the girl who had called. What was she doing in Grandma's house anyway? Everybody knew that the old woman had stopped seeing people years ago.

✳ ✳ ✳

Linnea strode out of the farmhouse toward the trailer where a group of girls had gathered to wait for their lesson. Elke was there, sporting a brand new pair of cream jodhpurs and a purple hoody. Her eyes lit up with malicious pleasure as Linnea approached.

"Ooh, look girls, it's Linnea! Back on our feet now, are we? Better not ride today 'cause otherwise we might have a fainting fit again!" Linnea ignored her and went into the tack shed. She grabbed the C.M. saddle and struggled back out with it.

"Thanks," laughed Elke, "but I'm not ready to ride yet." Linnea pretended not to hear and headed out toward the pony field.

"Hey!" shouted Elke, "Where are you going with my saddle?" Linnea didn't answer but quickened her pace. She reached the first field and let herself in.

"Hey! You!" Elke had now broken into a run, "Give me back my saddle!"

"It's not your saddle," Linnea shouted. She too had started to run but she knew that Elke would soon catch up with her. "It belongs to Carolina Malmgren, that's why it's got C.M. engraved on it."

"Right," said Elke who had caught up with her now.

She grabbed Linnea's ponytail and forced her to stop. "Carolina Malmgren is in a wheelchair, you idiot, so I don't think she's going to need a saddle, do you?"

By now Linnea had reached Moonlight's field and the beautiful pony was ready for her. Linnea hurled the saddle over the top of the fence, hoping for the best, and then she squirmed under the barbed wire.

"What are you doing?" Elke demanded as Linnea started to heave the saddle off the ground.

"I would think it's obvious," said Linnea, buckling straps. She eyed the barbed wire nervously. It was far higher than anything she had jumped before. She stroked Moonlight's neck.

"I'm serious," said Elke. "If you try to ride that pony, you'll end up like Carolina, or maybe worse."

"That's ridiculous," said Linnea. She squeezed her heels and set Moonlight at the fence.

Moonlight cleared the barbed wire easily and they cantered through the main pony field toward the road, but Ruth had seen them and she ran to the gate.

"Dismount at once!" she shrieked. "Dismount!" Linnea thought fast. Normally she would have led a pony onto the main road but she knew that if she did this, Ruth would have time to stop her. She patted Moonlight on the neck again, as a kind of secret signal, and then set her straight at the gate. Fortunately there was no traffic coming. Moonlight cleared it easily and they set off down the road toward Hemmerby. Linnea glanced over her shoulder and saw Ruth jumping into her car. This required a change of plan. Moonlight was fast, but she would be no match for a car.

Ahead of them came the fork in the road, right to Hemmerby, left to the village. Linnea directed Moonlight left and then swerved onto a little path that ran toward the sea.

"We're going to see a friend of mine," she explained.

To her relief Emmy was on the veranda when they arrived.

"What are you doing?" she cried in amazement.

"Hop on," said Linnea, "we may not have much time."

20: 56, Gullway

With Emmy's arms gripping her waist and the wind blowing in her face, Linnea had to concentrate on every bump and bend in the road. Although Moonlight moved swiftly there was plenty of traffic coming in the other direction. Linnea gritted her teeth each time a car approached. There seemed to be so much that could go wrong. What if Moonlight suddenly lost her nerve? This was hardly an ideal route for a pony with a checkered past. Was it even legal to ride two together on a busy road?

At first they made good progress and Emmy shrieked with excitement.

"I can't believe how fast we're going!" But as they came into Wisby a tractor laden with hay bales pulled in front of them and Moonlight slowed to a walk.

"Overtake," urged Emmy, "we've got to get past this thing." But then a large truck rumbled past in the opposite direction and Moonlight shuddered.

"Emmy, I'm scared to overtake. If this tractor's going to Hemmerby we'll lose too much time. Do you know another way?" Emmy nodded.

"Yes, when I'm on my bike I go along the railroad tracks."

"Well, we can't put Moonlight on a train, can we?" scoffed Linnea.

"No, stupid," said Emmy, "It hasn't been a real railway line for years. It's a bike path running along the coast."

"That'll do," said Linnea.

Emmy gave directions and soon they reached a narrow dirt path running between rows of cottages. They caught glimpses of the sea as they rode. A few sailboats were tacking against the wind toward the far side of the bay. Seagulls soared above them and the smell of salty seaweed lingered on the breeze. Apart from a few dog walkers who stood aside to let them pass, they had the path to themselves and Moonlight was noticeably more relaxed.

"This is much better," said Linnea with relief.

"What's the matter?" replied Emmy laughing, "don't you like living dangerously?"

Linnea looked over her shoulder. Emmy's red hair was fluttering in the wind and her green eyes were shining.

After twenty minutes the houses along the path began to get bigger and older and the gardens became more formal. Emmy guided them until they reached a long road leading toward a gas station. It was flanked with medium sized apartment buildings.

"Over there," cried Emmy, "56 Gullway." She slithered off Moonlight and ran to the doorbell.

"I'll stay mounted," said Linnea. "Ring as many times as you need to."

One ring was enough to bring a tall man to the door. His face was dark and craggy and he had unusually long arms which hung down by his sides.

"What are you doing?" he thundered as soon as he saw Linnea. "How dare you bring that horse here?"

Linnea's heart began to thump.

The man's face was twisted with pain. Linnea had hoped that arriving safely on this pony would do the talking for her. Now she couldn't think of anything to say.

There was a noise from inside and a girl in a wheelchair came out of the house. She was slim and boyish-looking with her grandmother's deep brown eyes. Her chin had a determined set to it.

"Milk-bucket?" she said.

Linnea dismounted and pulled the reins over the top of Moonlight's head.

"Come on, beautiful," she whispered, "now's your chance." Then she led Moonlight to her former rider. The pony seemed to know exactly what to do. With infinite gentleness she nuzzled Carolina's shoulder. Carolina lifted her hand and reached out to touch the pony, but then she changed her mind. This spurred her father into action.

"Go away. Both of you. I don't know what you think you're playing at. Just clear off. CLEAR OFF."

"No," said Linnea, "we won't." The words were out of her mouth before she had time to think.

The man's eyes widened at this new act of defiance. He looked furious and his neck was bulging and red.

"Go!" he screamed, "Now!" but Linnea held her ground.

"I'm sorry you're upset," she said quietly, "but shouting and screaming doesn't help."

"And what would you know about it?" sneered the man.

"My father was killed in a motorcycle accident last year," Linnea replied. The effect of her words was immediate. A hint of softness appeared in the man's eyes.

"I'm sorry, kid," he said, "it's just that this pony here…"

Carolina wheeled herself forwards.

"Let me feel her," she ordered, and this time she held out her hand. Linnea twitched the reins slightly and the pony buried her nose in Carolina's fragile hand.

"Which hospital did you say Grandma is in?" she asked. Emmy smiled triumphantly and Linnea felt the weight of the world fall from her shoulders.

21: Refusing Hurdles

If Linnea had gained any satisfaction from her trip to Hemmerby it faded as soon as she got back to Farhult. Ruth had telephoned Mom and the two of them were waiting for her at the entrance to the riding school. Linnea could see from halfway down the road just how much trouble she was in. She rode Moonlight up to the gate with as much calm as she could muster, but she knew that her horseback riding skills would cut no ice with Mom. The excitement of riding to see Carolina and proving Moonlight's worth had taken all of her energy, and as she dismounted she realized how exhausted she was. Ruth took Moonlight's reins and led her away. Mom took Linnea's elbow and marched her wordlessly back to the summer house. Then Linnea was sent upstairs to change out of her riding things. Sam and Anna were dispatched to the village with a long shopping list. They would be out of the way for at least an hour.

When Linnea came down to the living room Mom and Max were waiting for her. Mom looked steely and Max looked uncomfortable.

"Have I understood the situation correctly?" began Mom. Linnea shuffled her feet and looked at the floor.

"You have trespassed on riding school property and disturbed Eva Malmgren, who then had some kind of collapse. You then took it upon yourself to inform Anna, far too late in my view, and the emergency services were called out. You then stole a pony that you knew you were forbidden to ride. You rode the pony on the main road, ignoring Ruth who tried to stop you. Not content with putting yourself and the horse in danger, you then took Emmy, who is an inexperienced rider, along with you on the *back of the horse*."

A little trail of ants crawled toward the trashcan behind her. Linnea wished that she could shrink to ant size and march at the back of the line.

"This isn't like you, Linnea," Mom continued. "Is Emmy behind all this?" Her eyes narrowed with suspicion. "I don't know where her parents are and it seems her grandfather isn't up to the job."

Linnea felt something snap inside her.

"This was entirely my idea," she said. "Emmy came with me because she cares about Moonlight and she wanted to prove what I wanted to prove."

"And what *exactly* do you think you have proved?" asked Mom icily. Max moved uneasily in his chair.

"I have proved that Moonlight is safe. Not just safe but excellent. I have proved to the Malmgren family that they were wrong about the pony and they should forgive Mrs. Malmgren. Eva has been hiding away for ten years because of something that wasn't her fault."

"I think Linnea meant well," pleaded Max. "Perhaps we have said enough for now."

"Are you kidding?" stormed Mom. "Linnea hasn't begun to hear the end of this…"

Max stood up.

"I'm sorry," he said.

"Where are you going?" challenged Mom.

Max walked to the door. "This isn't my style, Karin." With that, he turned and walked out of the house. Mom followed him out as he climbed into his car.

"Wait!" she cried. "Where are you going?" But Max started the engine.

"I need time to think," he said, giving Mom a sad smile. Then he slipped the car into gear and set off down the driveway.

"When are you coming back?" asked Mom, but Max ignored the question, turned onto the main road and disappeared.

Mom ran into the house and Linnea's heart sank.

✳ ✳ ✳

The next day Linnea feared that she would not be allowed to go riding and she crept downstairs wondering what sort of reception she would get, but all the fight seemed to have gone out of Mom. She just sat in the courtyard cradling her coffee and looking defeated.

"Yes, go if you want to," she said wearily. Linnea would far rather have had yesterday's fiery Mom. She wanted to hug her and say, "Mom you were right. I have done dangerous and stupid things and I will never behave like that again," but she knew that she wouldn't mean it. Taking a chance with Moonlight had been worth the risk, especially if it had persuaded Carolina to visit her grandmother.

When she got to the riding school, Linnea was the center of attention. Ruth gave her a brief smile of acknowledgement and all the girls, except Elke, gathered around, eager for news.

"Did you really ride all the way to Hemmerby?"

"What happened to the lady? Is it true you saved her life?"

"Do you realize you could have been *paralyzed*!"

"Look," said Linnea, "it was no big deal. There's nothing wrong with the pony, okay?" She looked across toward Moonlight who had been taken back to her high-security field.

"Why has Moonlight gone back there?" she demanded, glaring at Ruth.

"Calm down, Linnea," said Ruth, frowning. "Even if there's nothing wrong with Moonlight, the other ponies aren't used to her. If we put her in the main field there might be a fight and I don't think she needs any more excitement, do you?"

Linnea was forced to agree. She remembered the rumpus that had occurred when Maggie had moved Nightshade into a field with Storm. The two of them had started biting each other's faces and necks. Linnea had watched in horror as they jostled and scrapped for supremacy. Storm had won, of course. You could tell that he would. He oozed authority, but it had still been a shock to see how vicious the power struggle could be.

"So I suppose you're going to ride the white nut-case at the Melmo Juniors," jeered Elke. Linnea looked at Ruth with pleading eyes.

"That's out of the question," said Ruth firmly. "Moonlight belongs to Carolina Malmgren. She's not a riding school pony. Linnea has trained on Holly, and Holly is the pony she'll ride." Linnea felt her heart sink to her boots.

"Linnea can have Pontus," said Emmy casually, "I'm not going to compete."

"Don't be silly," said Ruth. "I've already entered you for the intermediate jumps, although after your performance yesterday, I think you might be better off in the circus."

Emmy stuck out her tongue, but Ruth ignored her.

"The Melmo Juniors will be a bigger event than usual this year," she continued. "The Eastern Regional contests have been cancelled, so the Melmo organizers have invited them to join us instead." Linnea felt a wave of apprehension.

"Does that mean the Reingold stables are invited?" she asked.

"The East Hampburg place? Yes, of course. They count as the Eastern Region, don't they? Okay, go get your ponies everyone, we need to get started."

Linnea felt her throat go dry with horror. Of course, it would be great to see Pia and Else again, but Klara on Storm? Could there be anything in the world more humiliating than riding Holly against Klara on Storm?

Ruth had set the jumps in the birch grove at their highest settings, and she was eager to give her best riders as much practice as possible. Emmy, Philip and Minette were dispatched to practice trotting and cantering on the circuit track so that Ruth could concentrate on the advanced jumps. Elke set off first, relishing the chance to show off. Her long black hair was tied in the usual snake-like braid, and she wore dark gray jodhpurs and a black satin jacket. Linnea had to admit that she looked magnificent on Jasper. She paced him with mechanical accuracy, and he took each jump cleanly, gathering himself effortlessly after each one.

"Well done!" said Ruth. "If you keep up today's form, Elke, you could win the trophy."

Elke smirked and flicked her braid over her shoulder.

"Who wants to go next?" she asked, eyeing Linnea.

"Your turn, Linnea," said Ruth. "I think after your exploits on Moonlight yesterday, you might manage this."

Yes, thought Linnea bitterly. *I could do it on Moonlight, but I don't stand a chance on Holly, do I?*

"No thanks," she said hastily. "I'll watch the others go first."

"Alright," said Joanna wearily. She thumped her muddy heels into Vixen's flanks and set off at a leisurely trot. She took the pony through the jumps looking thoroughly bored by the whole experience.

If I had a pony like that, I'd give it a good run, thought Linnea, gazing at Vixen's strong hindquarters.

"Fine." said Ruth with little enthusiasm. "Now Edward. Your turn."

Edward seemed eager for speed. Linnea winced as he set Ash too fast for the first jump. She cleared it, but was flustered and brought the next two tumbling down.

"Alright, alright!" protested Ruth, "Go to the end of the line. I don't want to spend all morning mending jumps. Linnea, you go now."

To Linnea's despair, Ruth started to mend the second jump.

"Shouldn't I wait till you're out of the way?" she stammered, but Ruth didn't look up.

"Don't worry, Linnea," she said, "it will be fixed it by the time you get here."

Elke and Joanna laughed uncharitably and Linnea felt her blood boil. She squeezed her heels, and the lumpy Holly ambled toward the first jump and then paused to graze. There were more howls of laughter from Elke and the others. Linnea groaned and nudged Holly back to the start. Three times she set her at the first jump, and three times Holly refused. Linnea felt tears stinging behind her eyes. It was hopeless – embarrassing, depressing and hopeless. She swung herself onto the ground in disgust and started to drag Holly back to the main field.

"Where are you going?" asked Ruth. She was lying on her back under the third jump trying to straighten a misshapen strut.

"Home," said Linnea.

"But we haven't finished yet!" protested Ruth.

"I'm not going to ride Holly at the Melmo Juniors," croaked Linnea. "Forget it." And she stumbled through the field and toward the shed, tears streaming down her face.

22: Sam's Plan

When Linnea got back to the summer house, Sam was the only person around. He was scraping cracked paint off the living room windows, and sharp white flakes of it had settled in his hair. Linnea kicked the gravel angrily, uprooting clumps of chamomile that had sowed themselves in the driveway.

"Where's Mom?" she asked.

"Upstairs. Got a headache."

"Oh, great," said Linnea with exasperation.

"When's Max coming back?" asked Sam as he stabbed at a particularly resistant patch of paint.

"Don't know if he *is* coming back," said Linnea.

"*What*?" asked Sam. He stared at Linnea. "What are you talking about?"

"Look, Sam," said Linnea, suddenly irritated, "he was just a boyfriend, okay? Boyfriends come and boyfriends go. It's not like he owed us anything."

Sam's bottom lip trembled. "No!" he yelled as tears began to trickle down his face "You don't know anything!" He flung his putty knife on the ground and ran down the driveway.

"Where are you going?" Linnea called, but Sam had gone.

Linnea sank onto the sloppily painted green bench and leaned her head against the shed wall. She listened to the hollow tapping of a woodpecker knocking for insects in the trees behind her. She needed a drink but felt too heavy-limbed to go to the kitchen for water. A few wasps buzzed around the thin trickles of strawberry soda that had soaked into the rough grain of the table. They stuffed their heads into the crevices of the wood, searching for a few licks of sugar. The heat of the day had reached its peak, the lettuce that Mom had bought yesterday was wilting in the basket by the door, and there seemed to be no point to anything anymore. Why was it that the things you wanted most were the things you couldn't have? Like a decent pony? A happy home life? A gold medal and occasionally, just occasionally, for things to go right?

She heard a car approaching from the village. Maybe it was Max. He'd decided that he couldn't live without Mom, and that he was going to spend the rest of his life letting her tell off her children whenever she wanted. But a small blue hatchback pulled into the driveway instead. Linnea groaned.

Looking purposeful, Ruth strode over to Linnea's bench and set her riding hat down on top of the wasps.

"What's gotten into you?" she asked.

"Nothing," said Linnea stonily.

"Come on," said Ruth, "out with it."

"How can you ask me to ride Holly at the Melmo Juniors?" grumbled Linnea. "I'm sick of her. I'm sick of the whole thing. I'm never going to be a good rider if I don't get decent pony, so what's the point?"

Ruth sighed.

"Look, I know Holly isn't much, but I can't help the fact that you're the newest rider in the club. You'll have to make the best of it. Anyway, competing is what counts, not winning."

"You call that competing?" spluttered Linnea. "Sitting on a pony that won't move, being laughed at by everybody? Why can't somebody just give me a chance to show what I can do?"

"I'm sorry, Linnea, but you've got to change your attitude. Come for the experience, and come to support the other riders. It'll be a great day and you'll learn something just by watching."

Linnea didn't reply. She knew if she opened her mouth she would explode like a volcano.

"Good," said Ruth, "so that's settled. I want you to be at Hemmerby Riding School on Wednesday at nine o'clock sharp. We're meeting in the parking lot."

Linnea nodded. Anything to be left alone. Ruth walked back to her car shaking her head. Linnea got up and went into the kitchen to get some lunch. There was no sound at all from upstairs. She squirted thick lines of mustard and ketchup onto a hotdog and poured herself a glass of chocolate milk. Then she went outside again, hoping for a quiet moment in the orchard, but as she settled into a deckchair under the largest, shadiest tree, a battered pick-up truck pulled in. Sam was the first to hop out, followed closely by Emmy and Emmy's grandfather. The old man clutched his back and straightened up slowly, looking into the sun and grimacing.

"Foolishness," he grunted, "Pure foolishness." Then he laughed under his breath. Meanwhile, Sam and Emmy dashed into the house.

"Don't!" cried Linnea, "I think Mom's asleep." But they either couldn't or wouldn't hear, and a few minutes later they emerged with a startled looking Mom. Her skirt was ruffled and her shirt was creased.

"What's going on?" she asked, running a hand through her hair. "How long have I been asleep?" The she saw the old man and the truck.

"So you're Emmy's…"

"That's right," said the old man. "Now you hop in, my dear. I'm afraid these kids are not taking no for an answer."

"I see," said Mom, half-laughing now. "Well, all right." And she climbed into the truck.

"Sam?" called Linnea "What are you doing?"

"He won't tell you," said Emmy brightly, "and neither will I."

"Oh great," said Linnea, "so whose friend are you?"

But Emmy just gave her a mysterious look, hopped into the truck after Sam and waved as they set off.

23: The Melmo Juniors

Two days later the weather was wet; a low, dense drizzle blew in from the sea. Melmo Juniors would be a washout, and Linnea felt relieved. Maybe she wouldn't have to go? She dragged on her jeans and sweatshirt and slunk downstairs. Mom was already up, sitting on an upturned crate and reading the newspaper.

"Morning, Darling. All set for the competition?"

Linnea pretended not to hear and went to the fridge.

"Ruth says she wants you there at nine, so we mustn't be late."

"I know," Linnea replied.

"What's the matter, Lin?" Mom asked, looking up from her paper. "I thought you'd be excited. All the girls from Reingold are coming, too."

"Yeah, yeah," said Linnea listlessly. There was no point telling Mom how she felt. She'd only get a lecture on how lucky she was to be riding at all. Think of all the poor children in the world who never get a vacation, let alone a riding lesson, blah blah. Trying to explain these things to grownups was hopeless.

After breakfast, they put Linnea's riding gear into the

car. They also packed umbrellas and a ground cloth. Mom had made a thermos of coffee and a picnic which, knowing Mom, would contain too many sandwiches and not enough cookies. Once everything was ready, Mom sent Linnea to fetch Sam. He was playing his keyboard in the shed, surrounded by pots of smoky-smelling creosote. He had been carefully avoiding Linnea for days and refusing to answer any questions about his activities at Emmy's house.

Nobody spoke much in the car, and Linnea was grateful for the silence. She racked her brains for excuses not to ride Holly. Her leg hurt? Her tooth hurt? Her brain hurt? She had to find some way not to face Klara on Storm. Maggie must never see her ride Holly. What on earth would she think?

When they pulled up outside Hemmerby Riding School, the parking lot was already full of SUVs and horse trailers. Girls in jodhpurs were running in all directions, calling excitedly to each another while their parents waited under large umbrellas.

"Shame about the weather, isn't it?" grumbled one woman as she came out of a caravan with a clipboard. "This will really separate the sheep from the goats."

Yeah, and I'm a goat, thought Linnea bitterly. *A goat with shabby riding gear and an awful pony.*

The judges were already seated at a trestle table under an awning, and one of the organizers, a small red-faced man with a white moustache, was giving instructions through a loudspeaker:

"All riders for intermediate jumps, please take your starting positions."

Linnea felt butterflies in her stomach, and she pulled Mom's sleeve.

"Emmy's in this one!" she said, "Come on."

She dragged Mom and Sam to the front of the crowd. Emmy was at the start, looking flushed. She was in her best cowgirl pants and vest. She had also tied plastic carnations into Pontus's mane.

"Typical Emmy!" laughed Linnea. "They'll probably disqualify her on sight."

"She's nuts," said Sam.

Despite her appearance, or perhaps because of it, the judges had put her first to ride. She took the opening jump well, leaning forward and hanging on tight. Linnea smiled and thought how much progress she had made since the beginning of the vacation. Maybe even the mad dash on Moonlight had given her more confidence. She made the second jump look easy, and then she set Pontus at a good speed for the third. Linnea had never seen her so focused, but the fourth jump looked tricky. It was deep at the base and would need good pacing. Linnea could hardly bear to watch and squeezed her eyes half shut.

"She did it!" shouted Sam. "Wow!"

Emmy was into her stride now. The next few jumps caused her no trouble, and now she faced the final hurdle. Linnea knew from experience that the last jump was often the toughest, especially if you had managed a clean run up to that point.

"Come on, Emmy!" she cried. But Emmy didn't give Pontus enough time to prepare. He caught the bar with his back hooves, and it rolled off. The crowd groaned with disappointment and then clapped.

"A very creditable first performance," said the man on the loudspeaker, "Well done, Siv Blakely, Farhult."

Emmy raised one hand in a happy wave.

Someone tapped Linnea's shoulder. It was Klara.

"Hi," she said, "Maggie told me you'd be here."

"Yeah," said Linnea awkwardly. Klara was a slim girl with huge brown eyes, an aquiline nose and shiny, dark hair. She was half Spanish and looked it. As always, she was wearing a blue velvet riding hat. She could have posed for a fashion shoot right there.

"Maggie says you'll be the one to watch today," continued Klara, "so I guess Storm and I are going to have a challenge." She smiled and flashed a set of perfect pearly teeth.

"Oh, I don't think I'm going to be much competition," sighed Linnea.

Then the loudspeaker announced the Falabella Small Kids Race, and tiny children on even tinier ponies lined up at the start. Anxious mothers shouted words of encouragement, and dads danced at the edges of the track with video cameras. Linnea felt a lump in her throat as she remembered her first event. Dad had been there, of course, proud as punch to see his girl ride. Sam, still a toddler, had sat on Dad's shoulders to see the race. Linnea rode Ricky, her first black Shetland, and together they won silver. Dad made a little display case for the medal, and all houseguests were solemnly marched into Linnea's bedroom to admire it. The Falabellas ambled over the finish line, and their smiling riders were whisked into the arms of grandmas, grandpas and doting parents.

Sam, who hadn't been paying much attention to the race, started fiddling with his cell phone, checking for text messages. Suddenly, he yelped.

Grabbing Mom by the hand he said, "Mom, I need a hot dog."

"No, Sam," Mom protested, "I've packed a picnic. We're having it after Linnea's…"

"Hot dog," said Sam firmly, "Now." And he dragged Mom toward the stand, ignoring her objections.

"You're on next," whispered a voice behind Linnea. She spun around to see Maggie.

"Oh Maggie," she gasped, "I'm not riding today."

"My Linnea, not riding?" laughed Maggie. "Don't be silly. I've got Klara really psyched up for this one. Go get changed and show us what you're made of."

Linnea nodded dumbly and trudged back to Mom's car. She perched on the edge of the hood and wriggled into her riding gear. "It's okay," she told herself, "once Holly flubs the first jump, no one will bother watching me any more." Then she walked to the starting point where Ruth was holding Holly and smiling. *Maybe I'm just too competitive for my own good*, Linnea thought with a sigh.

"Elke Standish will open this event for Farhult Riding School," said the loudspeaker-man. "The riders are tackling a demanding circuit. May I remind you, no flash photography, please." A polite ripple of applause rose from the crowd, and Elke set off.

Jasper looked resplendent this morning. His chestnut coat gleamed through the fine drizzle, and he carried his head high. Elke had braided his mane and tail, and the old Liddington saddle had been polished and buffed for the occasion. Elke herself looked steely: her lips were clenched and thin.

She took the first jump with balance and poise. Then she took the next three fast, very fast. It was a high-risk strategy, but Jasper rose to the occasion. The fifth jump could have gone badly wrong. Jasper took the bend awkwardly and lurched at the fence. The crowd held its collective breath, but he survived. Elke looked rattled and slowed down so much that the next jumps looked labored, but they cleared them all the same. Linnea glanced at Minette and the rest of Elke's gang. They were clasping bags of chips and jumping up and down with excitement. It looked as if Elke was going to make a clean run. One last fence remained. Jasper gathered himself and went for it. It was a huge leap. You could see the power in his hind legs as he jumped. But his hooves scraped the top of the bar, and it slipped. Elke raced him to the finish, flushed with fury, and flung her riding hat to the ground. The next few riders were not distinguished. First, a tall black-haired boy made a bad start and only recovered for the last three jumps. His nerves had let him down. Then, a sharp-faced mother fielded her twins. They were dressed in matching blue outfits, and both of them looked anxious. The mother shrieked instructions from the side and succeeded only in distracting them. They both finished badly, having knocked down more jumps than they cleared. *But bad as they were, they finished the course, which is more than I'll do*, thought Linnea.

Klara was next. Storm looked like a king, glossy black from head to toe. How could you fail on a pony like that? He took the first four jumps smoothly. There were admiring whistles from the crowd. Then he took the bend that had confused Jasper and lined up for the next jump. He sailed over it. Airborne, he looked set to carry his dusky princess into another world. The next three jumps were as effortless as the first. Only the last one remained. Klara started to smile. Victory was surely within her grasp now. Again Storm flew into the air, but had he set off too early? For a fraction of a second he hung over the jump, and it seemed possible that he would clear it, but no. The bar fell. The crowd sighed, but Klara smiled elegantly and patted Storm's neck. It had been a good run.

"Elke Standish and Klara La Manga-Niepen are currently sharing first place. Now the final entry from Farhult," said the loudspeaker, "Linnea Karlsson, on Milk-bucket."

"What?" gasped Linnea, swinging around to face Ruth. "What's he talking about?"

24: Milk-bucket Rides Again

Ruth grinned.

"We got a message from Hemmerby Hospital," she said. "Apparently, Carolina and her grandmother plotted this during visiting hours yesterday."

Jonas Malmgren pushed through the crowd, leading the beautiful gray.

"You're j-j-j-oking," stuttered Linnea.

"Put your money where your mouth is," he said gruffly, handing her the reins.

Linnea's heart flew to her throat. She flung her arms around the pony's neck.

"This is your chance!" she whispered. Then she mounted and took three deep breaths to calm her beating heart. The jumps loomed out of the misty rain. She gazed at the red and white striped poles which gleamed like half-licked candy canes.

Linnea looked down and realized that she was sitting on the beautiful Liddington saddle. Jonas must have insisted on this, otherwise Elke would never have parted with it. There were no excuses now. She had a powerful and experienced pony, a world-class saddle and a circuit that would require all her skill. She smiled to herself. Cinderella had finally made it to the ball.

Moonlight was tense, waiting like a coiled spring. Linnea gave her a little squeeze and the pony bounded forward, eager for the first jump. She soared into the air and there was a murmur of excitement from the crowd. They landed cleanly on the far side, and Moonlight settled into a steady pace for the next one. The second jump passed beneath them, but Linnea wasn't aware of directing Moonlight at all. *How can this be?* she wondered. *How can you ride a pony and yet not ride it at the same time?*

Now they lined up for the third jump. It looked high. Higher than the barbed wire around the forbidden field? Higher than the gate out of the Farhult Riding School? Maybe. The ground beneath Moonlight's hooves was soft and sodden. "Please don't buckle," Linnea prayed. As Moonlight took off, she leaned deeply into the jump as Maggie had taught her. The crowd gasped, and Linnea realized that Moonlight had made an enormous leap. "Save yourself," she begged, "don't peak too soon."

Next came the sequence that had troubled Jasper. The fourth jump was a low cross, which seemed easy, but it came just before the bend into the fifth. Jump, slow down, hold the bend then up, up, up! She did it! Linnea grinned. Next came a two-stride double. Moonlight's footwork was as nimble as ever. Now a pyramid log-pile, solid looking and high. "Don't refuse it," she murmured, "smoothly forwards, take it in your stride." But Moonlight didn't turn a hair. Over she flew, and there were more hoots of admiration from the crowd.

Then as the final jump loomed, everything changed. Linnea could feel Moonlight tightening, tightening. His pace became frantic and his neck swayed and arched. *He's losing it*, thought Linnea in a panic. *This must have happened when he threw Carolin*a. Suddenly she had a vision of herself flying through the air like a rag-doll and landing in a crumpled heap. "No," she shouted with all her might. "Jump!" There was no room for hesitation, and Linnea was brutal. She drove Moonlight into the preparation zone and clamped her head so low that she was sure the pony could feel the heat of her breath. "Now!" she ordered. The next thing she knew they were both in the air, and Linnea steeled herself for the sound of a falling bar. Instead, the crowd erupted. They had made it. A clean run!

"A truly wonderful ride there by Linnea Karlsson," boomed the loudspeaker. As Linnea dismounted, Emmy dived into her arms. "You did it!" she cried, "You won!"

Ruth was there too, but Maggie got to Linnea first and lifted her off the ground.

"I knew you'd do it," she said squeezing her hard, "I said you would, didn't I? I only wish you'd done it for Reingold."

Linnea smiled. "Well, if you give me a decent pony next year, then maybe I will."

"Well, you've certainly got a decent pony there," said Maggie looking up at Moonlight. "Where on earth did you find her?"

Klara stood nearby, looking wistful.

"Well done," she said politely.

"Thanks," said Linnea, and she squeezed Klara's arm. Then the organizer called for attention.

"Ladies and gentlemen, as you know, it is traditional for the Red Pajamas to be awarded immediately. I would like to introduce a young woman who is well known in this region for her riding and for her courage; Carolina Malmgren." The crowd applauded and cheered.

"Well, go on," grumbled Elke pushing Linnea toward the judges. She walked across the damp grass as if in a dream. Carolina was sitting at the judges' table behind an enormous silver trophy.

"Well done," she said, holding it out to Linnea. "That was an amazing run."

"Barry Magnuson from Eastern News," said a small man in a mustard-colored raincoat, who was wielding a camera. "Stand next to Carolina and hold the trophy nice and high. That's it. Let's get some good shots for our readers. In a minute, I'll take a few of you with your pony."

"Oh," blushed Linnea, "She's not *my* pony…"

The photographer disappeared back into the crowd to get a different camera, and Linnea looked at the trophy. It was about twelve inches tall, and its handles were encrusted with silver flowers and berries. The sides of the trophy were engraved with lists of names and dates.

"Milk-bucket should have won this years ago," said Carolina, smiling wistfully. "But we just got a merit in the end. I'm glad she's finally won it with you."

"But…" began Linnea.

"Oh, don't worry," said Carolina, "It'll say Moonlight when we get the cup engraved."

"No, I meant…"

"Don't you want to see your red pajamas?" asked Carolina.

"My w-w-what?" stammered Linnea. What did Carolina know about the red pajama dream? What was going on?

"Look," said Carolina. She took the lid off the trophy and inside was a pair of doll-sized red pajamas."

"Don't ask me why they're there!" laughed Carolina. The trophy goes back to 1910, and nobody knows what the pajamas are for!" Linnea stared at them in amazement and shivered slightly.

"Now off you go to pose with Moonlight," laughed Carolina. "You're famous now!"

As Linnea walked back toward the pony, Mom and Sam ran toward her, and Mom swept her off the ground in a bear hug.

"Lin, darling, that was amazing! I had no idea you were such a good rider."

"Cool," said Sam appreciatively. "Better than your soccer." Mom took Linnea's hand and looked into her face.

"Have your photo taken, Lin, and then meet us back at the car. We need to get home soon. I've got news."

25: The Prize

The sun had come out by the time they reached the summer house. The air smelled clean, and raindrops sparkled in the apple tree like jewels.

Mom dried the green bench and poured three glasses of cola.

"So what is it, Mom?" Linnea asked. "What's the news?" Mom was about to reply when a pickup truck rumbled into the drive.

"Blakeleys!" shouted Sam, running up to greet them.

Emmy sprang out, followed by her grandfather and Ruth.

"Linnea, Linnea, I'm going to Montana!" she cried, running up to her friend and grabbing both of her hands.

Linnea tried to look pleased.

"When are you going?" she asked.

"For the start of the school year," Emmy replied. I'm going to live on the ranch and guess what? I *ride* to school!" Linnea nodded, trying to seem enthusiastic. Everything was coming to an end so quickly.

Mom poured glasses of strawberry soda for the guests and everyone accepted them gratefully.

"That was a great ride, Linnea," Ruth said. "I'm so glad you won it, because I forgot to give you this." She pulled a small gold pony charm out of her jacket pocket and handed it to Linnea. "From Eva," she said. "She's also written you a letter."

Linnea took the small white envelope and tore it open.

Dear Linnea, it began,

I'm writing this from Hemmerby Hospital, but the doctors say I can go home next week. I know what you're thinking, but it won't be like before. You've shown us that we were wrong about Milk-bucket and wrong about each other. So next summer you're on painting duty, and I'm going to inspect your work. Carolina and I have decided that Milk-bucket is yours from now on.

Linnea read this last line a second time.

We'll stable her at Farhult during the school year, but during vacations she's yours. You can't trespass any longer, because you're an honorary Malmgren.

Eva.

P.S. Hope you won the red pajamas.

"I don't believe it," Linnea cried. "She's given me Moonlight! But how can I …"

"Well, that all depends…" said Mom smiling. "Please excuse us, everyone. Linnea and I need to have a quiet word."

She took Linnea's arm and led her down the driveway toward the cornfield. Poppies flowered around the edges, and three sparrows pecked at some dust by the side of the road. The sun was lower in the sky now, and the corn glowed golden brown.

"Lin, I'm not quite sure how to ask you this, but Max…"

Linnea could see that Mom was nervous. She fiddled with her collar and pushed a small stone into the road with her toe.

"What would you say if…"

"Has he asked you, Mom?" Linnea prompted. "Has he asked you to marry him?"

Mom's smile was the only answer she needed. Linnea flew into her mother's arms and squeezed her tight. She felt such hope welling up inside her that she couldn't speak.

"So you approve?" asked Mom.

Linnea just nodded and pressed her head deeper into Mom's shoulder.

Mom rocked Linnea backwards and forwards as if she were a baby again. After ten minutes of laughing and crying they walked back toward the summer house, and Mom whistled. Max immediately crept out of the abandoned wing with cobwebs clinging to his hair.

"How long have you been in there? Linnea giggled.

"A while," laughed Max, "quite a while. Sam sent me a text about a gymkhana thingy that I couldn't miss. Then I ordered a round of hotdogs and somehow ended up proposing to your mother. That part was entirely Sam's fault, I might add." His eyes were twinkling now. "Then you won your race, and I was sent back here to hide for my pains. That's the trouble with beautiful women. They treat you mean." He smiled and took Mom's hand.

"He only came back because of Sam," laughed Mom.

"Sam deserves all the credit," agreed Max. "He sent me a very abstract swirly portrait of your Mom's eyes that made me see sense."

"So *that's* what you were all doing!" exclaimed Linnea, looking accusingly at Emmy and her grandfather.

"So now we can come to Farhult every summer," said Max. "What do you say to that?"

"Fine," said Linnea, "as long as we get to stay in a really classy, freshly-painted summer house next time." And everybody laughed.

✳ ✳ ✳

Later in the evening Mom, Max, Sam and Linnea sat down to a candlelit meal of canned tuna fish and stale rolls.

"I'm sorry, Max," Mom laughed, "in all the excitement I forgot to buy food."

"Yeah, no more special treatment," said Sam, "you're family now."

"This *is* special treatment," said Max gazing into Mom's eyes.

"Come on, Sam," said Linnea. She jumped to her feet. "Let's leave the lovebirds on their own for a while. I want you to meet my new pony…"